The Fakir of Florence

A novel in three layers

Paul Cudenec

Il fachiro di Firenze

Un romanzo in tre strati

Paul Cudenec

Winter Oak Press, Sussex, England, 2016

winteroak.org.uk

ISBN: 978-0-9576566-6-6

INDICE

THE SULTAN AND THE SAGE

One day while he was sitting under an olive tree, contemplating the earth, the sky and the dimensions of the cosmos, there came to the wise Perantulo a man on horseback. His face was obscured by a richly decorated silk scarf and he was accompanied by a dozen mounted warriors, whose scimitars glistened in the sun.

The man was none other than the Sultan of Khaluvia, who had received word of the teaching, the healing and the presence of Perantulo and wanted to see for himself this legendary fakir. The Sultan dismounted and approached the sage, unwinding his scarf so that he could be fully seen. He was plainly of noble character and had the look of one endowed with both intelligence and mental strength,

1

but Perantulo saw at once that there was much that separated him from Knowledge. Having ascertained that this was indeed the sage he had been seeking, and after whom he had been enquiring for many days, the Sultan looked silently into Perantulo's eyes and Perantulo looked silently and unflinchingly back. This moment stretched out until it became uncomfortable for the Sultan's warriors, who did not understand what was happening and longed for it to end. But none dared move so much as a muscle or utter so much as the softest of whispered sighs as the two men remained locked in mutual scrutiny.

Finally, the Sultan dropped to his knees and, with tears welling in his eyes, declared: "Never before, Perantulo, have I seen in the eyes of man or woman what I have just discovered in yours. I must confess that I have wondered these last days whether the rumours of your wisdom were not exaggerated by the loose tongues of gossiping embellishers, but now I know that their inaccuracy strayed in the opposite direction to that which I had feared to be the case. Your reputation does not do you justice, Perantulo, and I say this without having heard you utter one word or move one finger. I beseech you, O Holy Man, to show me how I can see what you see, know what you know, shine as you shine".

There was a long pause. Perantulo remained so still that a small green lizard walked up one arm, across the back of his neck, and down the other.

And then he told the Sultan: "It is a fine thing, O Great Ruler, that you have come here and spoken thus. Your people are fortunate indeed to be led by a man of your sensibility. But it is no easy thing you seek. The path is long and steep and you would do well to bear in mind the fable of the traveller who feasts on his supplies in celebration at having reached the lofty summit of his destination only to realise, when the mists lift, that he has merely conquered the lowest of the foothills that come before the plain that leads to the sea across which lies the mountain he would ascend".

"I know the path is long, kind sage. Fear not – the mist of impatience will not blind me on my journey," spoke the Sultan.

Perantulo waited for another long moment – moments for him bore little relation to the moments of ordinary men. He was so still that a golden butterfly alighted on his upper lip and preened itself for a while before fluttering on its way.

"Very well," said the old philosopher to the Sultan. "But you should know that the task ahead of you involves three stages. The first, which is quick and easy, is to express the Desire for True Knowledge. The second, which will be painful to you and to those who love you, is to rid yourself of all obstacles that can prevent the Torch of Eternal Truth from shining through you. This stage is dangerous for one whose commitment is not complete, for one who is not strong enough to bear the hatred of others or for one who is not supple enough inside to absorb the hurt. It is a dark voyage from which you may never emerge, O Sultan-most-Splendid".

The Sultan, a pensive frown creasing his brow, drew a deep breath: "And the third stage, O Holy Perantulo?"

"The third stage," replied the fakir, "can only be imagined when the first two stages have been completed".

The Sultan nodded. "So be it," he said. "I have understood".

And then he sprang to his feet, turned to his bemused men, and roared: "Let you all stand witness, my warriors, that your master, the Sultan of Khaluvia, today expresses his unquenchable commitment to the Desire for True Knowledge, that from this moment forth his days among mankind will be devoted to no other cause and that nothing and nobody can stand in the way of his Quest. Now we will ride, ride, ride – back to our famous City of Alzorika, which will soon become famed not just for its wealth, its learning and its arts, but for the devotion of its 75th Sultan to the Glory of All Being!"

He leapt on to his horse, raised his sword in the air as a sign of his energy and determination, then span to face the sage, who was still seated under the tree.

"Perantulo!" he cried, the fire of zeal scorching from his eyes. "Perantulo! I have heard your words and I will hold them in my heart! I will return!"

At that, he span his horse round, let out a mighty cry of inchoate resolve, and then he and his soldiers headed back off across the grasslands in the direction from which they had come.

During the Sultan's impassioned declaration, Perantulo had started to open his mouth as if about to speak, but had then decided against it. He watched the party disappear into the distance with the faintest hint of a sad smile upon his lips.

As he rode back to his palace, the Sultan said to himself: "Perantulo has warned me that this second stage will be dangerous and he alluded to the possibility that I will not go far enough in my efforts to remove all obstacles to the Torch of Truth. I owe it to him to ensure that I have heeded his warnings and I will not return to him to ask about the third stage unless I am sure that the second has been completed".

He resolved that every time that he felt he had achieved what had been asked of him, he would sit and imagine the old man sitting opposite him, listening to his account. The look in the eyes of the sage would tell him whether or not his efforts were yet sufficient.

When he arrived back to the domes, turrets and minarets of his magnificent capital city, the Sultan knew at once what he had first to do. He ordered his servants to clear the palace of all the sumptuous decorations of which he had always been so proud and to place them all under guard in the enormous covered market of Alzorika. Obeying without question, but with bewilderment written all over their faces, the servants pulled down lavish wall-hangings, carried off bronze statues and elegant urns, removed the golden medallions from the pillars of the Banqueting Hall and even, at the specific insistence of the Sultan, fished the rare multi-coloured fish from the fountain in the Courtyard of the Khaluvian Kings and took them away in glass tanks. There was only one wing of the palace that was exempt from the purge and that was the domain of the Sultan's wife.

When all the splendid items had been laid out in the market halls, the Sultan had his men invite the poorest people of the city – widows, cripples, half-wits, freed slaves, scavengers and water-bearers – to come to the halls and each take one item of their choice. Whatever was left was offered to the next neediest section of the population, until all was gone from the halls and distributed around the slums.

The Sultan did not need to consult his mind's image of the wise man to know that this was, in itself, not enough. He immediately instructed his cooks to prepare only the simplest meals for him and his court – the excess of fine meats, truffles, sugared almonds and honeyed delicacies from all corners of the Empire was to be disposed of as they saw fit. They were, however, to retain sufficient supplies to maintain the luxurious standard of living enjoyed by the Sultana and her immediate household, which included their two sons. The Sultan had no wish to incur her wrath and so far he had managed not to alert her to what he was doing.

As he pondered what his next move should be, the Sultan gazed into the fountain, which looked so plain and yet so pure without its former denizens. When he caught sight of his own reflection, he knew what had to do. He retreated into his quarters, took off his heavily-embroidered silken finery and ordered his manservant to fetch him a simple wool tunic of the kind worn by the lowest order of priests. He then had the contents of his wardrobe taken in ox-carts to the countryside, where they were handed out to the peasants tilling the fields and to the free men who eked out a simple existence in the great forests of the Pommonic Hills.

Alone in his stripped-out quarters, dressed in his plain tunic, he pictured himself telling Perantulo what he had so far achieved. The look in the old man's eyes was not encouraging. It seemed to reach straight past the Sultan to the palace in which he was standing. Even deprived of its lavish decorations, it was a magnificent building – and far too grand for a humble truth-seeker such as he aspired to become. He decided he would have to move out.

Just then, there was flurry of voices and footsteps in the hallway outside and the Sultan's wife, Yoloccina, came sweeping into the room accompanied by some of the leading dignitaries of the city. "What is the meaning of all this?" she demanded, waving her hand to indicate the emptied-out rooms of the palace beyond her own wing.

She was not happy and neither, it turned out, were the merchants and money-minters of the capital, who had been mightily offended by his decision to give away his riches to the poor. "Your Highness, do you not see that your most loyal and devoted servants, the cream of the empire who have worked hard throughout their lives to attain the high-ranking status they enjoy today, cannot fail to be hurt by your actions?" enquired the Master of the Ostan of Alzorika. "Were you to have distributed this great wealth equally among all your subjects, including those of the higher classes, their pain would perhaps be less severe, but to bestow your favours uniquely on the lazy, the inadequate, the lowest dregs of our society..."

The Sultan held his head in his hands.

Was this what Perantulo had been warning him of – the negative reaction of others to his righteous efforts? "Enough!" he shouted at length, interrupting a bitter complaint from the Guild of Master Butchers about the adverse impact of free meat on its members' takings. "Enough of all of this! I am the Sultan and you will not presume to tell me how to manage my affairs!"

Dismissing all of them except for Yoloccina, he then told her that he would be moving out of the palace forthwith and dispensing with the services of his personal staff. She was welcome to keep her own wing, but he, for one, would from now on be living in one of the small houses in the outer grounds built 50 years ago to house the mercenary soldiers who came to fight in the Great War of the Razor's Eye and which were kept empty and waiting in case there was ever need for such visitors to return. When he refused to listen to her objections, she stormed off, crying that she would never so much as look at him again so long as she lived.

A terrible mood of self-doubt overcame the Sultan as he sat in his sparse new home, all alone and contemplating the bowl of spiced chick-peas and the chunk of coarse black bread that was to be his evening meal. All the eager-to-please faces that usually surrounded him were gone, his two sons were out hunting so could provide no company for him, and even the mealtime absence of the Sultana, difficult woman though she was, left an empty feeling in the pit of his stomach. What sort of life was this for a Sultan?

With that thought, he leapt to his feet. Of course! That was the core of the problem! Why hadn't he seen that before, rather than worrying about the surface details of his regal life? It was his Sultanship itself that was the obstacle to the Truth. He called for his legal advisors and within an hour had signed a document ceding his title to his elder son, the traditional heir. He himself was no longer the Sultan, but Askush – the name by which he had been known as a young boy. The new Sultan and his brother were due back to Alzorika at any time now, so although the deed was done, he would delay the general announcement until he had spoken to them.

Askush broke the news to the two of them together and they both received it with barely a flicker of emotion crossing their faces, as befitted their station. But when he spoke to each of them in turn, on their own, a different picture emerged. The younger lad was upset not because he himself would not become Sultan, which he had no reason to have expected while his brother was alive, but because he feared it would alter the relationship between the siblings. He felt that the older lad had often sought to gain an advantage from his greater experience and the fact that he was heir, and that, while they had reached an agreeable equilibrium of late, his sudden succession to the throne would bring out the worst in him. There was a tear in the lad's eye as he reflected that the hugely enjoyable hunting trip from which they had just returned could well prove to be the last occasion on which the pair would spend time together on an even footing.

For his part, the elder son was not pleased to be inheriting his father's mantle so soon, it appeared. He had always known that one day the privilege and responsibility would be his, but he had hoped, in all frankness, to have enjoyed the carefree days of his youth without the serious obligations involved in being Sultan. Since his father was not yet old and was in evidently rude health, he had not mentally prepared himself for the assumption of this burdensome role.

Despite it being impressed upon him that the legal transfer of power had been completed, he begged his father, with tears in his eyes, to reconsider his decision.

When they had both departed, Askush collapsed on to his simple bed. He felt completely drained. How had he managed to create so much unhappiness by following a path with the worthiest of intentions? When he thought of the tears of those two strong young men, who had been so close to his heart for so many years, he himself began to sob and to sob, filled with a perplexing mixture of remorse and confusion.

In a while he fell asleep, but was rudely awoken after less than an hour by a hammering on his door and windows and a great hubbub in the street. Half the city seemed to be outside his new home and they were screaming their frenzied hatred of the man they had now been told was their former Sultan. He was a coward, they were saying, a weak-willed traitor who had let down his faithful people. Peering out of a small upstairs window at the crowd, Askush noticed several members of the disgruntled merchant classes whose dissatisfactions he had learnt of earlier in the day. But the great majority of the mob consisted of the common people, the poor – the very ones who had benefited from the disposal of his wealth. He understood that the merchants must have been busy whipping up anger in order to gain the support of the very classes they despised, but he still could not help feeling a crushing disappointment that the people of Alzorika had turned against him.

The angry mood finally wore itself out for the evening and people started dribbling away, shouting that they would be back in the morning. When he was sure they were all gone, Askush crept out, made his way to the stables, saddled his horse and rode away into the night.

It took him three exhausting days to find Perantulo, who had moved on from the olive tree where they had last spoken. There were moments when Askush felt like giving up the effort of searching and just riding off somewhere else and forgetting the whole thing. In his heart, he wanted to go home, back to the life he had known, but it was too late for that now. Askush felt exhausted by what he had experienced since he had last spoken to Perantulo. He felt that he had lost everything that he had ever had and that he had aged at least twenty years in just a few days. But at the same time he felt consoled by the knowledge that he had done what he had to do. By the time he finally reached the sage he had managed, despite all the sadness eating away at his heart, to enthuse himself with the thought that now that the second stage was complete he would be entrusted with knowledge of the third stage that lay ahead.

Perantulo was seated on a stone in the middle of a small river, his legs dangling in the water. He seemed to be completely absorbed in watching the ever-shifting patterns in the flow of the stream and the rippling of reflected sunlight shimmered and eddied across his lowered face.

"Good day to you O Perantulo!" declared the dismounting horseman.

"Good day to you, too, O Askush!" replied Perantulo, not even raising his eyes.

Askush was astonished that he had addressed him by that name, but resolved to say nothing about it and to continue with his account as he had composed it in his mind, regardless of whether the old man somehow already knew of all that had passed.

Somewhat breathlessly, he told Perantulo every detail of what had happened to him in Alzorika, confident that he had surely achieved all that was possible in his bid to complete the second stage and rid himself of all obstacles that could prevent the Torch of Eternal Truth from shining through him. The third stage would soon await him and sweep away the trauma of the terrible sacrifices he had just made.

When he had finished, there was a long silence while Perantulo sat calmly on his stone in the river, gazing into the flow. He was so still that a great silver fish leapt from the water onto his lap, gobbled up a fly that had landed there, and then wriggled and plopped back into the stream.

Finally, he raised his head and spoke. "Askush," he said. "Your account fills me with me with great gladness for you have now successfully achieved the first stage of the journey on which you have embarked – by your actions you have indeed expressed your Desire for True Knowledge. But now, my friend, comes the second stage and here your real effort must begin".

STRATO CONTEMPORANEO

1

I've reached the end of the platform and I'm just about to cross the concourse of the *Stazione di Firenze Santa Maria Novella,* in a relaxed mood and quietly looking forward to my stay in the Renaissance capital, when something a bit disconcerting happens. A man suddenly appears out of nowhere, careers clumsily into me and, without pausing for a moment, let alone apologising, dashes off again towards some other platform.

It all happens so fast that I don't really get a good look at him. He's roughly my age I think, maybe slightly older, and of similar build. He's even dressed in much the same way as me, although in a state of some disarray. His black shirt appears to have been smeared with white paint, one of his trouser legs is ripped and covered with blood and the small rucksack he's carrying is gaping open at the top, with some of the contents bulging out as if he had tried to break the world record speed for packing before setting off to the station.

As I watch him disappear into the crowd, he turns his head for an instant and looks back at me and in that face I see two things. Firstly, that he does indeed look like me – or, at least, a sort of haggard and eccentric caricature of me. Secondly, that he is afraid of something. His face looks clammy and pale, his eyes animal-wide and alert to danger. What exactly he's scared of, I have no idea. Missing his train, perhaps? Sometimes people become so obsessed with the immediate detail of their everyday lives that it strips them off some deeper equilibrium and inner calm that could be theirs if they could only step back and look at themselves from a certain distance.

I take this peculiar incident as a timely reminder of the need to keep up a Zen-like level of detachment while I am here, so as not to end up like this wretched pseudo-doppelganger and his soul-eroding angst.

It doesn't take me long to regain my poise and good humour as I amble across the concourse and take in my surrounds. There is something a little magical about other countries' railway stations. I always go and have a look if I find myself in a foreign city. I like to see how it's all laid out, where the people congregate, where the departures are listed, what sort of ticket desks and machines are available, where it is that people can drink a coffee or buy a paper. I particularly like reading the lists of destinations on the boards. Firstly, there are the places you have never heard of, satellite towns and suburbs served by local commuter trains. Then there are the towns and cities whose names are familiar, but in a different context. For you they are exotic places, far-off places, places that belong in the atlas of your imagination. Suddenly, here, they are real places, mundane places, places that are 40 minutes away, served by three trains an hour, and whose names thrill nobody. Thirdly, there are the international destinations. For those of us used to living on an island, there is still something remarkable about this. At St Pancras International the trains through the tunnel to Europe are quarantined from the rest of the station – it feels more like you're walking into a mini-airport. But elsewhere, "on the continent", these supernatural border-breaking metal serpents slither in and out of the station among all the local bustle without anyone so much as raising an eyebrow.

Can you really get a train direct from Paris to Madrid? Is it truly possible to hop into a carriage in Rome one evening and get off again the next morning in Bavaria? Yes it is, although you might be disappointed if you had anticipated arriving in Monaco, as in the glitzy sun-kissed

Mediterranean principality, rather than Monaco, as in the Italian name for solid and rain-sodden Munich!

In addition to my general fondness for railway stations, I particularly like Italian ones. There's usually a certain feeling of style, of *eleganza*, of space, of an underlying solid calmness beneath the *treno*-travel-trauma.

So I am a little disappointed to find that following signs for the exit leads me through a small and slick spendzone that could have graced any of the great cultural centres of the world like the Mall of America in Bloomington, Minnesota, the Al Salaam Mall in Jeddah or Gatwick Airport's fragrant South Terminal.

I like to travel in a state of relaxation. I would always rather arrive somewhere two hours ahead of time, rather than risk the stress of being ten minutes behind. So when I gave my hosts in Florence an estimated arrival time at the station I added in a bit of leeway, for my own peace of mind, just in case of any delays and missed connections. A lot of leeway, in fact – my traditional two hours' worth.

This is fine, as it gives me an opportunity to have an initial look at some of the city, before I am whisked off to their home for the evening. I travel light, so my rucksack's not a problem to carry around.

I escape the clutches of consumerism, brave

the terrors of traffic – although incurring the horn-pummelling wrath of a very large bearded man in a very small bright-blue car – and slip off the main road into what looks more like the Florence that I was expecting, and which I distantly remember from my one previous visit 25 years ago. Five minutes into a jumble of narrow streets, there is a slight opening-up of the ancient urban density and into sight comes the rough and unadorned facade of the *Chiesa di San Paolini.*

I am clearly "meant", by the mighty compass of destiny, to go inside and so I do. After a moment or two getting my bearings, I realise that the inside is not as old as I expected. However, it's still pretty impressive. At the far end of the nave is a massive carving of Christ on the cross, with behind him a many-rayed sun that looks from this distance like a perspective-flattened palm tree.

Turning to look around me, I am immediately drawn to a remarkable pair of sculptures. On either side of a tomb are two skeletons, caught in the act of climbing out from under black shrouds. This is not a symmetrical arrangement, since they are both doing so in slightly different ways – one has his left arm stretched out and is lifting the heavy cloth with his right hand, while the other is already partly sitting up, his left hand pulling the shroud away from his head and his right hand not visible at all.

"Lifelike" doesn't seem the right word to describe this gruesome scene, but I am struck by the way that they are not merely symbolic skeletons, but individual skeletons, each with his own personal way of rising from the dead. I can't help reaching for my phone and taking a snap of this veritable gem of grotesquery.

A little further into the church is a confession box, its purple curtain hanging limply on the middle of the rail. Above the box is wooden carving of an angel's head and wings and above that a portrait of a thoughtful-looking man in some kind of cowl. I quickly snap another shot of the painting and move on.

Another confession box, another purple curtain, another angel, another portrait. This time a woman, who may be a saint or even the Virgin Mary. Again I press the photo button, only to wonder what I think I am doing. Do I really imagine that I will gain anything from converting all of this into digital format and saving it on my mobile phone? I know I'm not going to send these images to anyone and I probably won't even look at them again, unless I have to fill in a minute or two waiting for a train or something.

By taking these photos in a church I'm becoming one of those people I've always scorned, one of those witless idiots who thinks they can actually *own* and keep hold of a piece of art, or a city skyline, or a beautiful landscape, or a moment in their lives, by saving an inadequate visual copy. What hubris! They go home and show their precious pictures to their parents and their neighbours and anyone spineless enough not to tell them to fuck off. This is *my* holiday. This is what *I* saw. This is *my* photo of Michelangelo's or Leonardo da Vinci's or Albrecht Dürer's work of art and don't you think that some of the credit, just a little vanity-teasing quantity of credit, should go my way for the skill with which I framed the shot, with which I carefully selected the subject matter, with which I walked up to it on *my* legs and saw it through *my* eyes, with which I went to that place, planned my holiday, earned the money to pay for it by surrendering my days to a salaried servitude made bearable only by the annual vacation-of-the-bowels-of-boredom during which I somehow persuade myself that I am not a zombie-moron but a living human being, a participant in life-and-culture-and-nature-and-history, by capturing and keeping and *possessing* as much of it as I possibly can with this little electronic gadget that I was clever enough to buy?

No, I'm not one of those people. I put my phone away and resolve to take no more photos in Florence. I want everything that I see and hear and taste and smell to sink into *my* memory, not my SIM card's. I want it to lose its form, its specificity, and become absorbed into my flesh. I want it to become part of me and I want to become part of it. I want the border between us to melt away and let loose a glorious interflowing of subject and object in which I can no longer even tell what is Florence and what is me.

I wander slowly back towards the station to await my hosts. High up on the front of the *Santa Maria Novella* basilica, above the exotic pointed arches, circles-within-squares and architectural scrolls, is a triangle containing a sun-disc and at the centre of its undulating rays is a face. It's the face of the sun, in a design that occurs time and time again in alchemists' illustrations but now takes pride of place on the front of an important Christian church. What kind of *alchimia* will this mysterious city work on me, I wonder?

I am brought to the flat where I am to stay for the next month. It's on the second storey of a solidly elegant 19th-century curve around the outside of a busy *piazza*. My room looks more like an office than a living space, which appropriate enough since I intend spending a lot of time working here. A broad white desk, two single beds, two chairs and a spacious wardrobe sounds ample for any room, but this space is so large that these contents still leave it looking empty. The walls are painted in plain pale yellow, there is an unused marble fireplace and the floor covering – which in fact runs through the whole flat – gives a very good impression of a Roman mosaic. The highest of imaginable ceilings is decorated with a well-mannered fresco which has a rose-robed cherub as its centrepiece and is bordered with little circular portraits of a couple of children and two matching paintings of wealthy-looking women in long blue dresses.

I shut the twelve-foot tall windows to keep down the traffic noise from the road below and head for the kitchen to get myself a glass of water. At the heart of this palatial *appartamento* is a big dining room which is also, in fact, the entrance hall from the stairwell and lift. Across the other side is the kitchen, which looks out on to the area between these apartments and the shops and flats round the corner in the next street. I walk on to a small balcony, which boasts a little rack of washing lines decorated with clothes pegs and dish cloths and is home to a stepladder, a pot plant and a shopping-bag-on-wheels.

The confusion out here is in stark contrast to the clean simplicity of the inside of the flat. The space between the backs of the surrounding buildings might be best described as a Canyon of

Chaos, a splendidly organic and haphazard collision of terracotta roofs, balconies, stairways, greenhouses, verandas, pipes, ducts, chimneys, pot plants and trellises. Beyond is the back of a newer and taller block of flats festooned with washing, the top of a palm tree, aerials, rooftops, and, in the very distance, one of the tree-covered green hills that surround Florence. All of this below the rich blue Italian sky.

Right down on ground level, at the bottom of the valley, I can see an outdoors sink which looks as if it may be at the back of a shop or restaurant. People wander out from time to time for a smoke. I peer straight down from the balcony. In an emergency, it would be easy enough to clamber your way down there, via all the various bits of roof and extension, I conclude. This is always good to know.

* * *

All places have a particular energy of their own, even if sometimes that energy is difficult to sense, because it's so deeply buried beneath the shops, multi-storey car parks, roundabouts, one-way systems, burger chains, multiplex cinemas, offices and factories of the modern townscape.

I find that the countryside always has a tangible feel to it, even if it's just a sense of peaceful calm. This is only destroyed by the intrusions of industrial life – the roar and stink of a motorway slicing right through it, for instance, or a long queue of hideous metal-giant pylons defacing the once-pretty slopes of some downland coombe.

The energy I draw from the countryside, from nature, is primal, raw, beyond words. That is its power, to lift us out of our human subjectivity, with all its blinkered limitations, and drop us into a reality that is so much older, broader, deeper, stronger, wiser. I can find the same kind of energy, even more intense in terms of time and dimension, by looking up at an unclouded night sky. The blue sky was an illusion: here is reality in all its unimaginable vastness.

Town-energy is different. It depends on the town, of course. Small towns or villages in the countryside tend to depend on nature for their energy. Part of their identity is simply that of the hills, mountains, fields, forests, lakes or rivers that surround them. Even the biggest cities are still greatly influenced by their geographical nature – think what the River Thames means to London, or the Seine to Paris, the Golden Horn to Istanbul. All such built-over places still have rivers, hills, valleys and seas through which a specific nature-energy seeps into them. And even without them there would still be the climate, the prevailing winds, seasonal patterns – this is all as much a part of any town's identity as its architecture or population.

But there is something else, as well, in the big towns. There is the energy-field given off by the humanity that lives there and has lived there. We all know that this exists, even though we may find it hard to explain exactly what it is. How else could we describe a middle-class English suburb as "sleepy"? Do we need to see people literally sleeping in deck chairs in their gardens to reach this conclusion? Why is somewhere else "edgy" or "exhilarating"?

The energy of a city does not just come from those who live there now, but is the accumulated energy of everything that has ever gone on there, all the lives that have been led, the thoughts that have been thought, the dreams that have been dreamed. Somehow this energy is connected to the physical structure of the city. Perhaps old buildings are the catalyst by which this invisible layer of meaning can enter our minds. Not necessarily old in terms of substance but in terms of shape, position, geometry, the effect that they spark in us. If an old town is reduced to rubble in a war and, in its place, a new modern town is built which bears little relation to the original place, it will be difficult to make contact with the previous spirit of the town, without looking at old photographs and pictures, reading historical accounts, talking to people who remember it. But what if the old town is restored to look the same as it used to – like Nuremberg in Germany for instance? Somehow the medieval energy remains tangible, despite the break in physical continuity.

Very old cities can have a multi-layered energy to them that really grips a visitor. I once spent a few days in Palermo, in Sicily, for example, and could virtually reach out and touch the richness of the accumulated layers of Palermo-ness, embracing multiple cultural influences from Arab to Norman, Phoenician to Roman, Punic to Greek. Palermo is still Ziz and Balarm in the same way that Istanbul is still Constantinople and Byzantium – despite the fact that both are big bustling traffic-choked modern cities.

This energy, although linked to a town's history, is not dependent on our knowledge of that history. You are not going to tune in to the soul of a city just by reading all the guide books, traipsing around all the museums and tourist sights. Ideally, a sense of the energy should come first, before the facts. It should inspire, prompt and focus our interest in historical fact. For a tourist, that is never possible. All has to be more or less simultaneous.

A lot of this energy, I would say, is absorbed on an unconscious level. Like radiation, it seeps into us without us being aware of what is going on. Who knows what effect it will have, what resonance it will find within us? Who knows when that resonance will come to the surface and in what form? What would it mean to be inspired with the spirit of Budapest, or Lisbon, or Mumbai? Does that place-energy bring specific ideas with it, or the capacity to embrace specific ideas? Does it activate or open up some part of our mind, reconnect us to a part of the collective human soul from which we were previously cut off?

I know it does something, because I have felt it myself, on numerous occasions. I feel improved, broadened, enriched by my encounter with the energy of a particular city, particular kinds of cities.

That is why when I was offered the opportunity to spend a month here in Florence, teaching English to some friends of friends, I immediately accepted. I had no particular intention of revisiting Florence, having "ticked it off the list" some 25 years earlier, and the direction of my reading and interests have not been leading me particularly towards Florence, or indeed towards Italy in general. But I know that Florence is a city with strong energy and that in four weeks some of that energy will have passed into me in some way or another. What this energy will be, and where it will lead me, I don't know and this makes the prospect all the more enticing.

Part of the reason why I have come to Florence is that I am free to do so. As a writer, I can work pretty much anywhere, given a steady supply of coffee. But I have no fixed ideas as to what exactly I am going to be writing while I am here. I have a number of projects in the pipeline, which I could easily get on with. One of them is a series of interviews being conducted by email with a French acquaintance who's interested in, and somewhat critical of, my work. My correspondent is very quick to get back to me with a follow-up point, or the next question, so I'm sure I could fill up my whole time here with this stimulating exchange, which we aim to publish online, and perhaps also in print, at some indeterminate stage in the future when we feel the conversation is complete. That prospect worries me a little, in truth, because I suspect it would also mean the end of a relationship which has become quite intense on an intellectual level. I've only met this person a couple of times and I don't really know how much we have in common on a more mundane level. What brings us together are the ideas in which we take a common interest, even if our perspectives differ. The day that we declare our online conversation (the "interview" aspect is just an excuse, really) to be over is thus also the day that we jointly agree that we have nothing more to say to each other. Where else could we go from there? Exchanging chit-chat about friends and places we don't share? Swapping links to blog posts that we suspect might interest the other person? That would be a sad step down from the intensity of our ideological sparring-match.

Maybe we could turn the tables and I should interview them about their ideas, instead? That would be strangely compelling. I've a feeling, though, that it would amount to the same text as their interview with me, just arranged differently. In fact, I could probably create something from what we have already exchanged, without ever mentioning to them that they were being interviewed. A stealth interviewer, who masquerades as the subject of the interview in order to glean and assemble information on the unsuspecting questioner. I like that idea. The end result would be strange entity, straddling a line between truth and lie. It would be fake in that no such interview ever took place. The exchange would be a fabrication, the wording often invented to carry the reversed direction of the dialogue. But essentially, if I constructed it in good faith, it would be true. It would be an authentic representation both of their views and of mine, as revealed in the original interview. It would potentially be as good as a real interview with this person. Possibly even better, strangely enough, as my interviewing technique might not have been so persistent. I might not have brought out so many nuances of differentiation between our respective positions, might not have elicited the subtle revelations regarding their own position that my interviewer was led to make while challenging mine. I like this idea as well. Fiction, if fashioned from the raw material of authenticity, can turn out to be truer than fact.

If the interview process doesn't satisfy me, I always have the option of going back to an essay I am writing on the subject of time. I've started it already, but somehow ground to a halt. That's the funny thing about writing. Sometimes it all just flows out, for day after day, as if it is all already there in your head – or maybe in the collective imagination – and is just waiting for you to make yourself available to write it down. You sit down in front of the computer, with all the time in the world available, and it seizes the moment to descend from the ether into the physical, or at least electronically-physical, form of words, sentences and punctuation. You are not quite a spectator to the process, because your brain has to be sufficiently sharp to form the language, but the content is very much present from the word go.

On other occasions, such as with the essay on time, it is all much slower. I am thinking as well as writing, finding my thoughts through words, rather than finding the words to express my thoughts. This isn't a worse way of working, just a different one. Maybe the writing here is taking place at an earlier stage in the development of the finished product. On other occasions, when the ideas come rushing out, it's because they've been gestating for some time, maturing in the alchemical vial of the mind where they have been nourished by a drip-feed of reading, reflection, conversation and experience until they have grown so big that they are gripped with the urgent desire, the absolute need, to be born into the light of day. But with the slower form of writing, the creative process is taking place on the outside, as it were. In the head rather than the belly, the conscious rather than the unconscious. Ultimately, though, their source and validity is the same.

It is perhaps because of this slight impatience with the slower form of writing I have recently been experiencing (there's an irony here, in the essay on time needing so much of it to complete), that another notion has arisen concerning the work I might get done during my month in Florence. Maybe I should start something afresh, something that belongs to my stay here. It's not that I think the subject matter will have anything to do with Florence, but that I might get some kind of inspiration from being here. This could be provoked by any new surroundings, I suppose, so those offered by the home city of *il Rinascimento* seem potentially to be even more fruitful.

I decide to wait and see. To "play it by ear", as so often seems the wisest course. Perhaps if I start writing something – anything! – it will gradually be infused with the spirit of Florence and turn into something quite different from what it initially appeared to be. A self-transforming text. All I have to do is to keep the words flowing and consciously-unconsciously leave the back door of my mind open for some new revelation to come bursting in with much trumpeting and delight.

* * *

I am in the *Piazza del Duomo* in the middle of the afternoon, looking up at the cathedral and letting all its complication and embellishment flow through my optic nerve into the cranial sedimentation tank where eventually I hope to make sense of it all.

Marbled in white, green and pink, it somehow has something of the seaside to it, a faded and bleached-out seaside, and this strange impression is reinforced by the huge shells washed up by the high tide under the roof. Limpet-domes cling underneath the massive red-brick octagonal centrepiece. Balletic balustrades and giant eye sockets. Dagger-sharp lancet windows and psychedelic spiralling sun disc. The geometry of order and the soaring of desire are interwoven, interfused and interrogated wherever the eye comes to rest.

It's all so overwhelming that I decide to simply cut it out of my mind and listen instead. You can tell a lot about a place by its sound. More than you'd think, even when there's nothing obvious going on like the lapping of waves, the roaring of a waterfall or the staccato machine-gun fire and blood-curdling screams of a ruthless massacre.

The first thing I can hear is the whining of an electric tool from a building site next to the *Duomo*. This is very much the dominant layer of sound and it takes a while before I can reach past it and pick out anything else. Behind that is a general hubbub of voices, occasionally catapulted into the foreground with a phrase that is not necessarily intelligible but at least identifiable as belonging to some specific tongue.

The rattle of a *bicicletta* across the flagstones. The drone of a *ciclomotore* skirting the *piazza*. The clip-clopping of a horse-and-tourist-trap. A woman's voice speaking Italian. The whooshing of a street-sweeping vehicle. The ding of a bicycle bell. A woman's voice speaking American. The murmur of distant traffic from beyond the *piazza*. The squealing of bike brakes.

A woman's voice speaking Chinese. The click-click of a metal walking-stick. The light trundling of a wheeled suitcase. A woman's voice speaking German. A man laughing back. Is the laughter in German, too? The purring of a car parking on the edge of the square. It stops. The rumbling of trolleys transporting slabs of stone into the works area, accompanied by the jovial shouts of the workers. The rustling of paper as a tourist consults a map on the bench beside me. The chinking of a little pile of metal as someone scuffs their foot against a chain coiled up beneath a roadside post. The clatter of a pushchair and a small child's voice, in Italian.

A hammering from the building site brings with it the echo of another hammering from the past, when the master masons and journeymen and apprentices were lovingly piecing together the great Gothic gift to the future that is the *Cattedrale di Santa Maria del Fiore.* Many of them may have worked on nothing else throughout their lifetimes, seeing that 140 years elapsed from the day in 1296 when the foundations of the masterpiece were dug until the completion of its crowning glory, Filippo Brunelleschi's *cupola.* More hammering, more chiselling, drifts across the centuries as the town grows up in the centuries before the *Duomo.* Gradually, the workmen's voices are shedding their Tuscan dialect and moving into the language of empire. It is 80BC and Fluentia is being built by Lucius Cornelius Sulla to house veteran Roman soldiers. Before that, two rivers flow together amidst the hills and forests. I can't hear the water from here, or any birdsong.

The reversing beep of a buggy-like vehicle manoeuvring in the *piazza*. A reverberating crash as someone bumps into the metal fencing around the building site. Male and female Italian voices. Another ding of a bicycle bell. The jangling of keys as a workman puts them back in his pocket. The tooting of a horn. The almost-inaudible sigh of a young woman who has just stopped to rest on the bench beside me. The road-sweeping lorry coming past again. The click-click-click of a tourist's camera. The sound of the zip on my rucksack as I put away my notebook and pen and prepare to move on.

* * *

I have had another idea for what to write while I am here. There has been a piece brewing in my head for a while now about the recuperation of radical ideas. About how, slowly and almost undetectably, an idea that's dangerous to the status quo can become infected with certain assumptions or outlooks of that same status quo and end up becoming part of it and indeed reinforcing it.

I think this has quite clearly happened to what might loosely be termed "radical" or "left-wing" ideas. There are so many instances where something promising seems to be happening, only for the new movement of ideas to turn into an updated version of what it was supposed to be opposing. The Protestant rebellion against the Roman Catholic Church is a good example. Luther can only really been seen as radical for a short period of time – after that he turned into a dictatorial monster calling for popular uprisings to be mercilessly crushed. It hardly needs pointing out that the Russian Revolution went the same way, fairly rapidly. But there's a background there which is less spoken about, which stems from the way that Marxism had already accepted industrial capitalism and worked for a revolution *through* that system rather than in opposition to it. In power, it therefore carried on with the factory-exploitation familiar from the capitalist world. In places where it was out of power and ostensibly a revolutionary force, its pro-industrial outlook meant it spurned the most powerful weapon available to any anti-capitalist movement – people's instinctive, deep-seated dislike of capitalism and the world it brings with it, and their longing for a different way of living. This proved disastrous in Germany at the start of the 20th century, where the left's failure to inspire and recruit those who would naturally rally to an anti-capitalist, anti-industrial message left them as easy pickings for the fake anti-capitalism and fake anti-industrialism of the power-hungry Nazis.

* * *

I have wandered into the *Piazza Santa Croce* and am thinking about going into the basilica, but it doesn't seem to be open. Instead I head off up one of the cool, yellow-painted narrow side-streets that criss-cross the old city.

There is a delirious diversity to so many of the buildings. Thin, tall houses wedged in between wider, lower ones, a multi-layered jumble of red roofs topped with satellite dishes, loft windows, iron staircases, tiny doorways, balconies, plastic chairs, flower baskets and copious greenery, including vines and rows of shrubs-in-tubs, trimmed into neat bobbles and spires. Below are four or five storeys lined with windows of varying shapes and sizes, all fitted with brown or grey slatted shutters, some of which can flap outwards at the base, forming the perfect pigeon ski-jump.

As I weave on and off the pavement to avoid traffic, parked cars, the occasional other pedestrian and the ubiquitous cyclists, I am aware that I am passing various little workshops tucked in among the tenements. In one of these I catch sight of an ancient car, nearly as old as me, with its bonnet open and its engine in dismantled disarray. Another is filled with a great mess of tubes, the sections of giant ducting all tangled around each other like a seething nest of enormous serpents. A rational observer could only assume that these devilish snakes, probably conjured up by some Saracen conjurer to lay waste to Christendom, were frozen into stillness by a benevolent Florentine magician a very long time ago, which is why they are covered in centuries' worth of thick grey dust, but that there remains the danger they will one day reawaken and take to the streets, leaving behind them a terrifying trail of turmoil and tears. The owners should pull the shutters down, just in case, I tell myself.

On the corner of the next street is one of the little religious shrines that litter the city, a painting of Mary and an arrangement of flowers, all covered in glass. Just a few feet away is some stencilled street art showing a figure with a television set for a head and the message, in English: "Let us think for you".

Eventually I emerge into a *piazza* hosting some kind of semi-permanent bric-a-brac market in its centre, consisting of four or five rows of wooden booths surrounded by trees. The aisles between the sheds are protected from sun and rain by a ramshackle plastic veranda half covered with a green substance that is presumably moss.

Before venturing into the middle, I circle the outside of the market area, which is rimmed with green, slightly decayed, railings, to which are chained dozens of bicycles. Like most of the bikes I have seen here, they are not in the finest of shape. Many have ripped saddles and display various botched attempts at repair. One *bicicletta* boasts a seat which seems to have been fashioned entirely from brown sticky tape. Its neighbour is missing both handgrips and its frame is eaten away by rust.

At one corner of the inner square is an automatic photo booth of the kind which in Britain is only ever found indoors, in shopping malls or railway stations. Here you can get your *fototessera,* an artless self-portrait ideal for identity cards and all the other many requirements of officialdom. At another corner stand two phone boxes which smell, in compliance with age-old and worldwide human tradition, of piss. Between them and the railings is a heap of old plastic roofing, alongside a useful stack of cardboard and a mould-infested single mattress.

I wander over to the huts to take a look. The first one I come to is offering a selection of paintings – mostly of fruit – together with a padded stool, a decorative table and lampshades.

The next displays several sets of cups, a statuette of a she-wolf, a candelabra, three pairs of spectacles and painted toy soldiers representing several centuries of militarist glory.

Opposite is a *stand* which specialises in larger objects – tables, chairs and heavily-framed paintings. It also hosts four huge urns – big enough to hide in, they have come straight out of Ali Baba's legendary cave.

In the next aisle I find more of the same. There is a box of antique dolls, of which one is black and one is a clown. There are vinyl records, earrings, vases and old postcards.

Sadly the booth advertising *libri usati*, second-hand books, the only items I am ever likely to buy at a place like this, is closed. But I am pleased to discover, as I emerge from the market area, that there is another book stall on the edge of the pedestrianised street.

The stall is in the form of a small wagon, which has been unfolded to reveal rows of crammed shelves, and a couple of auxiliary trolleys. A canvas awning on the top has been pulled open to guard against any threats to the reading matter emanating from above – whether that be rain, sun, pigeons or the angry pointing finger of some thin-skinned patriarchal deity unhappy with the way he has been depicted in one of the volumes on sale.

I can see from a distance that these are likely to be the sort of books I am interested in. Despite the wisdom of the popular saying, the cover of a book is often a handy way of assessing its likely contents. There must be some relationship between the imagined readership of a certain kind of book and the sort of cover that publishers imagine will appeal to that kind of reader. This might have nothing to do with their actual preferences and exist solely in the minds of the publishers, but it still results in a definite style of cover that can instantly be recognised by those interested, or uninterested, in reading material of that description. Perhaps it's got nothing to do with appealing to specific visual tastes at all, but is just a code that has been established over the years, convenient for all concerned. Cheap crime thrillers will look like *this*. Swooning sentimental romances will look like *this*. Eccentric pseudo-intellectual novels will look like *this*. Nobody has to waste their time in closer examination of books they're not the slightest bit interested in. They can head straight for the right kind of aesthetic – the right colours, the right artwork, the right typeface – and find the satisfaction of entering a reading-reality in which they know they will immediately feel at home.

The stallholder is a tall, slim man in his late 50s, wearing tinted glasses, a grey cap, a black t-shirt, grey shorts, white socks and half an inch of grey stubble. When he sells a book he reaches into the pocket of his shorts for any necessary change and then, with the lick of a finger, separates a little plastic bag from his supply, flicking it open deftly with one hand before placing the purchased item within.

I walk over and a closer inspection reveals a fine collection of books on Aztec Civilization, Egyptian Civilization and Islamic Civilization; books by Plato, Aristotle and Nietzsche; books of poetry, photography and prayers. There are lots of books about Florence, lots of books about art and almost as many about both. I am tempted by a couple of these, but there's no point in buying them as I'll have no room in my rucksack to take something of that size home with me when I leave. It is partly with that consideration in mind that I pick up one of the smallest titles on offer and partly, of course, because I am drawn to the cover, which features an old portrait of a thoughtful-looking lightly-bearded man with a bloody dagger piercing his chest. The title is *Il fachiro di Firenze*, which I have difficulty in deciphering until I read the blurb on the back and get a bit of context. Of course – *fachiro* is fakir. *The Fakir of Florence*. That has a certain ring to it. The content is intriguing, too. A strange wandering sage turns up in Florence just as the Renaissance is getting underway and finds himself accepted and then rejected by the Medici-led metaphysical milieu behind the creation of the Platonic Academy in the city. Leafing through, I see that the book also includes transcripts of "sermons" delivered by the *fachiro* during his years in Florence. I have heard neither of the historical character at the centre of the book nor of the author, one Paulo Diacono, but it looks like just my sort of thing. And, as a clincher, it only costs one euro.

I take the book over to the stallholder and he smiles as he takes it from me. "*Una bella storia!*" he comments, which could mean "a beautiful story" but "*storia*" also translates as "history", which is what he obviously intends here.

When he sees the translating cogs turning in my head, he switches to English: "This book is very particular," he says. "Is published next year".

I laugh. "I'd better hurry up and read it before it comes out then!" I quip loudly enough to satisfy my need not to let the mistake go unremarked and yet quietly enough that he doesn't feel the need to reply.

"Ah!" he grins and raises a finger in the air. With a lick and a flick, he pops the book in a plastic bag and I'm on my way.

When I get back to the flat, I peruse the pages. It is a semi-academic book, with incomplete references in footnotes. The original

15th century stories told by the fakir, and written down at the time, are interspersed throughout the main narrative. Since the book begins and ends with these stories and they appear regularly throughout, they give the impression of propping the whole thing up, like seven biblical pillars of wisdom.

I switch on my laptop and look for some information about *il fachiro* on the internet, but I can't find anything. I return to the book and peek at little segments here and there. I sample one of the sermons in its entirety. I want to start it properly from the beginning, but it will soon be time for the English conversation session and, after that, dinner.

Normally, by the time Italian meal-time is over, I am too tired to do much in the way of reading and am more or less ready to fall asleep, but tonight is different. I have been itching to start the book for hours now, and I waste no time in arranging myself in a comfortable and well-lit position and getting underway. Some hours later, in the early hours of the morning, when I finally close the volume, my eyes are tired but my brain is still wide awake. And one specific, marvellous idea has taken hold of it. I could translate this! The subject matter seems to be almost unknown, and yet strongly appeals to me. The book is a new one, though I can find no date in it, and certainly won't yet be available in English. It would be a great test of my linguistic ability and also a good challenge for me to get stuck into over the next month.

The next morning, I take a short post-breakfast stroll and then get straight to work.

STRATO STORICO

I

At around 10am on Monday November 7, 1459, an unkempt, brown-skinned and long-haired stranger emerged from the shadows of a narrow side-street and strode into the autumnal sunlight of the *Piazza del Duomo* in Florence.

His ragged clothes – a rough woollen tunic and brimless cap – would have marked him out as a beggar, probably attracted to the fabulous wealth of the Tuscan city which was at this time pretty much the centre of European civilization. He stopped below visionary architect Filippo Brunelleschi's great red-bricked *cupola*, to which the finishing touches were still being made, put down his small bundle of belongings and began to address the morning crowds. There was nothing unusual in this, as preachers were as commonplace here as anywhere else in fifteenth-century Christendom. The content of his message to the citizens was, however, certainly out of the ordinary. One eye-witness, quoted in Matías Vecino's authoritative history, recalled: "He spoke well, but with an accent that seemed to come from a place and a time very far away from our city and his discourse, too, echoed that impression of absolute incongruity. He was a messenger come to us from the stars".[1]

Unfortunately, the exact content of this first Florentine sermon has not been preserved and we can only speculate as to its nature from the evidence of the teaching which has been passed down to posterity. However, it was certainly of sufficient originality to attract the attention of the above-cited bystander, who turned out to be a key witness to the astonishing historical vignette which was now to be played out.

Sandro Cellini was a young man, of humble origins, whose insatiable appetite for learning had led him to become a pupil of Giovanni Argiropulo – known to the English-speaking world as John Argyropoulos. The Greek scholar was one of the leading figures in the rediscovery of classical knowledge and thinking in western Europe that became known as the Renaissance.

Cellini, like so many others, had been thrilled to attend the lectures delivered in Florence by this product of Byzantine culture, who had been born in Istanbul – Constantinople at the time – some 44 years previously and had now sought permanent refuge in Italy after the fall of that last bastion of the Eastern Roman Empire to the Ottomans in 1453.

The young student was, however, now even more spellbound by this stranger's preaching and seems to have fallen into a kind of trance, from which he was only roused two hours later by the ringing of the noon bells across the city. He realised he had been completely distracted from the errands he had planned to carry out that morning, but these now seemed of little consequence in the light of what he had heard. Looking back later on what it was that had so appealed to him, he saw an important continuity with the philosophy in which he was already immersed. The stranger's address to the people of Florence had suggested to him "the spirit of the teaching I had learned from Argyropoulos, if not the letter". He explained: "Here, I felt, were the ideas of antiquity which had so inspired me, but set free from the confines of the written word and the carefully constructed philosophical argument. I felt I was touching something primeval, drinking from the source of the river of thought on which I had set sail. If Aristotle, and through him Argyropoulos, represented the brains of this perennial human wisdom, then this stranger seemed to me to embody the heart. If Aristotle was the sun, here was the moon".[2]

He resolved on the spot to bring together these two aspects of what seemed to him to be the one philosophy and, as the stranger picked up his affairs and prepared to move on, young Cellini rushed forward and took him by the arm. He praised him for his speech and urged him to come and meet others of his acquaintance. We do not know if Cellini specifically mentioned Argyropoulos, but this was evidently in his mind. At first, the stranger resisted and even, it would seem, physically pushed Cellini away from him.

He said that he was merely passing through Florence and would now be on his way. The Florentine public had not appeared particularly interested in what he had to say and he would waste no more time on them. According to Cellini's account, he also insisted that it was not to the philosophers of Florence that he wished to speak, but to the common people of Tuscany. He declared that he had little in common with the "bloated babblers" of the city and preferred the company of peasants to that of the "parasites of power".[3]

Somehow, though, Cellini managed to persuade him to stay in Florence. He took him back to his parents' house across the river in the working class area of San Frediano in Oltrarno, where he was fed and offered a bed for an after-lunch nap. We do not know what Cellini's family made of this eccentric foreigner, but there is nothing to suggest he made any kind of adverse impression.

While the stranger slept, Cellini hurried back across the Arno and made enquiries as to whether Argyropoulos would be prepared to receive the visitor. The 20-year-old was very much a student of the Greek academic, rather than a colleague on equal footing, and it took some effort to get the request through to his mentor and to receive a reply. To his delight, the answer was positive, and Cellini rushed back home to fetch his guest.

As he approached the *Piazza Santo Spirito*, he was surprised to find a crowd had gathered.

Working his way through the throng, he saw that the preacher had taken up position on the steps of the half-built new church and was entertaining the assembled onlookers with a story about a stork, a volcano and a fig tree.

Here, the stranger had perhaps found the ideal audience for his unorthodox ideas. Divided by the water from the administrative core of the city, this was the area in which had emerged the beginnings of dissident intellectual thought in Florence. One of these early groups, in the previous century, had gathered around Giovanni Boccaccio, author of *The Decameron*[4] and a student and friend of Francesco Petrarca – better known simply as Petrarch – who had in fact stayed at Boccaccio's home here.

The metaphysical rebellion that flourished first in this part of Florence – the challenging of narrow Christian certainties with the reintroduction of classical pagan thinking – was mirrored in physical rebellion. Indeed the church of *Santo Spirito* itself is said to have been a rebel stronghold during the *Tumulto dei Ciompi* (Ciompi Revolt) of 1378 – one of the earliest attempted working-class insurrections in European history.[5]

So it was a potentially fertile ground on which the preaching stranger cast the seeds of his oral wisdom and by Cellini's account there was an immediate rapport with the crowd which had not been in evidence in the wealthier surrounds of the *Piazza del Duomo*. There was a story-telling element to the foreigner's approach that seemed to have captured this public's imagination and, even when Cellini reached the steps and managed to whisper in the speaker's ear, he had a hard time in dragging him away from his appreciative audience.

The preacher promised to his *Santo Spirito* listeners that he would return – which he did on many occasions – and allowed himself to be led away by a no-doubt over-excited Cellini to his appointment with Argyropoulos.

The student is a little reticent in his account of what exactly transpired during the meeting of the two older men whom he held in such high regard. The end result was satisfactory – the Greek expressed an interest in the newcomer's ideas and seems to have more or less invited him to become a member of the philosophical circles in which he moved.

However, had he expressed more enthusiasm than that, we can be sure that Cellini would have reported it, and we can only assume that the scholar had some initial reservations about this character to whom he had just been so hurriedly introduced.

Argyropoulos was, after all, a serious man with a serious reputation. He was a university professor, gave private tuition on Plato, translated the works of Aristotle, published Plotinus' *The Enneads*. He was steeped in the scholarly detail of classical knowledge. While Cellini may well have appreciated the breath of fresh air blown in by the foreigner's informal approach to metaphysics, Argyropoulos would not necessarily have felt the same way, being very much inside the walls of Academia, such as it was at the time. We can imagine that it would have been difficult for him to know how to react to the preacher. This man was not presenting himself as a student and was at least as old as Argyropoulos himself, and yet neither was he a contemporary of his in the field of philosophical study, nor an authoritative figure to whom he could look for guidance.

One surprising revelation did serve as a slight bond between the two men – their paths had crossed before. It transpired that the stranger had spent several years in Constantinople and had survived the bloody conquest of the city by the Turks by hiding for three days in the cellar of an abandoned monastery until a repentant Mehmed II called an end to the brutal slaughter and destruction.

The stranger described having attended a talk on Plotinus delivered by the Greek scholar a few years before the Muslim conquest and in particular recalled a heated debate between Argyropoulos and one of his audience on the distinction between essence and existence as laid out by the thinker and writer known to medieval Europeans as Avicenna, but who was in truth a Persian polymath of the Islamic Golden Age called Ibn Sina.

Argyropoulos remembered the occasion in question, to which he had referred in correspondence[6] and was intrigued to discover that the stranger had been present. In fact, in a letter from that period (to Bendetto Ambrogini), Argyropoulos seems to refer to his first meeting with the preacher, referring to "an unexpected echo of a distant incident in the words of a peculiar traveller".[7]

If the companionship that one might have expected to see between the two exiles from Byzantium did not immediately materialise, this was perhaps because they did not altogether share the same culture. Although the stranger had lived in the city on the Bosphorus for several years, he was not a native of that place. They spoke to each other in Greek for part of the time, but Cellini reported after the meeting that Argyropoulos had commented on the other man's unusual accent. This implicit invitation to provide some biographical background was not taken up by the newcomer.[8] The element of mystery concerning the stranger's origins, while it must have added to the initial fascination that he evoked among the Florentines, was ultimately used against him by those who became his enemies, as we will see later.

Cellini and the stranger therefore left the Greek scholar's rooms without having established the strong connection that the student had possibly envisaged, but the visit was far from being without consequences. Through his meeting with Argyropoulos, the preacher was in turn to be introduced to someone with even more influence, who would draw him into the very heart of Florentine culture and intrigue.

1. M. Vecino, *Il Rinascimento e l'apocalisse,* 1954.

2. Ibid.

3. Ibid.

4. V. Branca, *Giovanni Boccaccio: profilo biografico*, 1977.

5. G. Di Leva, *Teatro. Il tumulto dei Ciompi, Firenze 1378*, 1972.

6. M. Badelj, *Giovanni Argiropulo e le origini dell'umanesimo*, 1948.

7. Ibid.

8. Vecino.

THE LESSON AT THE TAVERN

Early one morning while Perantulo was wandering in the hills south of Beziz he was caught in a violent thunderstorm. Spying a village ahead, he quickened his pace through the deluge in the hope of finding shelter. He was heading for the temple, where he had thought to escape from the rain for a while, when he spotted a great hollow yew within its grounds.

"Ah!" said Perantulo. "What better resting-place for a man of my kind!" and he curled up in the dry interior of the ancient tree and fell asleep.

When he awoke, an hour or so later, it was to the voices of three earnest young men, deep in conversation outside the temple.

He climbed out of the tree and went

over to them, carefully avoiding the many puddles and little streams of water left over from the storm. After they had greeted each other, and Perantulo had explained a little of the calling in life that brought him so far from the land of his birth, the most forthright of the young men said to him: "It is a stroke of good chance for the three of us, O Sage, that you have arrived in our humble village at this moment, for you may be able to help us with this dispute concerning the destiny of our souls".

Perantulo nodded and agreed to listen.

"It's like this," said the first young man. "My friend here, Walil, follows the teachings of the School of Farzib and insists that when our current existences end, we are each of us reincarnated in some new-born creature or person. I, on the other hand, am a disciple of the School of Lezzam-Lezu and am certain that after death, our souls are united in the Superior Realm and freed from all confines of earthly existence". Perantulo nodded again and turned to the third fellow, asking: "And what is your view of the matter, young Sir?"

The other two laughed and the lad looked a little embarrassed as he said he didn't know.

"Humik has no opinion," said Walil.

"That's why Koffu and I are discussing all this again for the seven thousandth time – each of us is trying to persuade him of our approach. He spends his days tending goats and eating wild figs and really hasn't got any views at all on these weighty matters".

Koffu and Walil both chortled merrily at the expense of the little goatherd, whose eyes betrayed a certain hurt at being thus humiliated in front of this erudite stranger.

A stern look flashed across Perantulo's eyes. The look was so severe that a small cat, sleeping in the shade beside the temple, woke up and splashed off through a puddle with a plaintive yelp.

"I think," he said, "that we should discuss this at the village tavern, always such a convivial location for the most important of conversations. Pray lead the way, my young friends!"

When they had taken a seat outside the tavern, Perantulo had the keeper bring a large jug of the finest red wine available. The innkeeper was a suspicious, mean-spirited character and, looking at Perantulo's simple clothes and ungroomed appearance, doubted whether he would have the means to pay. His distrust was so strong that it burst out of his narrow little mind and made itself known to Perantulo, who headed off any ill will by immediately proffering a silver dinar which would more than cover the cost of the refreshment.

The youngsters, being of humble background, were not accustomed to such good living and their tongues were dry in anticipation of the expensive wine. But when the innkeeper brought four glasses for the drinkers – the best he could lay his hands on, since the old stranger had paid him so handsomely – Perantulo immediately took two of them and wandered off to the other side of the street. His companions strained their necks to see what he was up to. He seemed to be scooping up muddy water from a puddle into the wine glasses!

Indeed, he now returned slowly and cautiously to the table bearing the two glasses filled to the very brim with filthy rainwater and placed them in front of Koffu and Walil.

"Now," he said. "Who would like some wine?" He started as if to pour some for Koffu and Walil, but could not do so as their glasses were already full, so instead he poured a healthy dose into the empty glass in front of Humik.

All three young men looked completely confused.

"And now," said Perantulo. "To the subject of your dispute. Koffu, you are right to say that beyond its individual existence, the soul is united with all others".

"Yes!" exclaimed Koffu, slapping his hand on the table and grinning gleefully at Walil.

A stern look creased Perantulo's brow. The look was so severe that a baby started to cry, far far away on the other side of the village.

"But at the same time as being right, Koffu, you are also wrong!" he said firmly. "You are wrong to think that it is freed for ever from the obligation of earthly being. Yes, there is a glorious moment when the individual spark is reunited with the flame of the whole, but the separation from material existence is momentary and there is still living to be done in other forms".

"Exactly!" burst out Walil, with a triumphant glow. "Don't you see, Koffu? We are reincarnated, time and time again!"

A stern look passed over the brow of the Holy Man. It was so severe that a cloud passed over the sun and the birds stopped singing in the trees.

"Walil," said Perantulo. "You are young and you have much to learn". And with these words his mood lifted, the sun emerged from behind the cloud and the birds resumed their song.

"Both of you," he said, calmly and kindly and looking at each of his listeners in the eye one after the other, "have had your minds filled with the muddy water of incomplete and corrupted doctrines, preventing the glasses of your intellect from being filled with the wine of Knowledge. More than that, you have now accepted so many of the false assumptions of these doctrines that it will be difficult for you to be able to receive Truth within the shape of those modes of thinking".

He reached out and seized the glasses in front of Walil and Koffu, one with each hand, emptied out the dirty water on to the ground and then flung them down, shattering them into hundreds of pieces.

The innkeeper peered out from indoors and cursed to think that the extra profit he was gaining from the silver dinar had just been dramatically reduced.

"The soul after death is no longer a thing that follows the rules of this world," said Perantulo, "in the same way as these glasses have lost the form which rendered them of use for the drinking of wine at this tavern. The idea of time is an idea of this world and relates only to the way in which our individual existence forms part of the Eternal Whole. It is the means by which we can subjectively understand and experience the extent of our individual existence, but that subjectivity no longer exists when the subject has died. It therefore makes no sense at all to speak of what becomes of the soul 'after' death".

The three youngsters looked at Perantulo. The bashful Humik was taking a first sip from the glass of wine that the old man had poured him. The other two looked uncomfortable and the sage saw that they had not yet understood.

"It makes no sense O Koffu, Disciple of the School of Lezzam-Lezu, to talk of us being cut off from physical reality in a Superior Realm," he said, "because we remain part of what is, always has been and always will be the reality of the entire Universe. And it makes no sense O Walil, Student of the School of Farzib, to talk of us undergoing a series of reincarnations, because we are already part of what is..."

At this point Perantulo's voice trailed off, as his words were taken up by the simple goatherd. "Because," Humik was saying, with a look of deepest delight spreading across his young face, "we are already part of what is, always has been and always will be the reality of the entire Universe!"

Perantulo smiled, poured himself a glass of red wine, downed it in one gulp and then said farewell to the trio, leaving the village behind as he headed back off on his travels.

Later that night, as the tavern-keeper slept, the silver dinar wriggled its way out of his purse, jumped aboard a shaft of moonlight and shimmered its way back to its master.

STRATO CONTEMPORANEO

2

Florence is not the best place to be for someone who finds obsessive photography a severe annoyance. Crossing the *Ponte Santa Trinita* I am forced to weave my way past tourists taking pictures, mainly of themselves. The new fashion, of which I have remained blissfully unaware, is for taking these "selfies" with the aid of a special stick, helpfully offered for sale by dozens of young black men haunting the riverside area. I have even seen this ritual being performed in front of the altar in a church. Never mind actually looking at what they have presumably come here to see – instead they'd rather take a photograph of their own over-red and over-fed British, German or American features leering fatly and triumphantly into the camera lens and all but obscuring the supposed object of attention which they have now succeeded in "owning" by photo-proxy.

I look up the river towards the *Ponte Vecchio*

and the higgledy-piggledy little buildings tacked on to it, on either side of the central three arches. It reminds me of drawings I've seen – a model, even, perhaps – of London Bridge centuries ago. But that medieval world seems so far away from the reality of London in the 21st century. Here, it is still present. The little streets and alleyways, the fading facades, the hidden courtyards – all of that is somehow part of life still. In England as a whole, it strikes me, the past appears dead. Even where the old buildings and streets are still there, they've too often been turned into a shallow imitation of themselves. They're too clean, too renovated, too much a product of the Tourist Industry. There is no sense of the sacred. How else could an American coffee chain be allowed to dominate the entrance to Canterbury Cathedral? Why else would every opportunity of sensing the resonance of an English past be blighted by gift shops, tea rooms, car parks and a general aura of gawping, gullible, cash-splashing ignorance?

Yet another party of tourists trails by, in the wake of a bored-looking bearded man holding aloft a green tour-guide flag and reciting his script in unconvincing English. Florence is hardly immune from tourism, I remind myself. This is a strange place from which to condemn my home country on that score! And yet... for all their photo-foolishness, the tourists here don't seem to have succeeded in killing off the atmosphere, the soul of the city, in the same way that is too often the case in England, where any place possessing an iota of historical charm, from Polperro to Pooley Bridge, has been turned into a kind of static amusement park, an historical off-motorway service station adorning the fringes of the real focus of attention, which is a massive over-priced car park for the conveyor-belt hordes of motorised "visitors" desperately searching for some kind of inspiration to light up the TV-numbed stupor of their hapless half-lives.

The past, in the UK, has been turned into a commodity, a product, a thing to be bought and consumed. It's been taken out of everyday life, separated from the people, scrubbed up clean and put on display behind a sheet of museum glass, behind a ticket desk and a 40-minute queue. The "past" is on sale here, too, in Florence, for those who want to pay. But it's a waxwork of the past that they sell to the foreigners who know no better. The real soul of Florence is still at loose, unchained, unpackaged, unrenovated and you don't have to spend a single euro in order to gaze at it, to breathe it in, to touch it, to walk on it and around it, to hear it, to sense it.

This is very clear on the south side of the river, a part of the town that is slightly less frequented by tourists, although just as old. Directly opposite the celebrated splendours of the

Uffizi Gallery sits the perfect illustration of how, for all its tourist-magnetism, Florence has not yet been sanitised, secured and sterilised in the name of Hygiene and Heritage.

Costa dei Magnoli is a little street that climbs up away from the Arno through an archway under some buildings and later joins *Costa San Giorgio* on its way up to *Forte Belvedere*. The first thing you notice is some street art on the wall of this covered section. A skull marked with a dollar sign, holding a bible and wearing Caesar's laurel crown, is raining bombs down on the flaming earth below.

A six or seven-storey edifice, of indeterminate age, connects to the buildings across the road via the archway, which itself consists of several floors. At the top of this in-between zone is a sort of railed rooftop garden. As I watch, a woman emerges from a doorway on the right and walks across. Below that are closed windows protected by wired grills, with weeds growing out of the base. The fabric of the wall is flaking.

On one side of the road the yellow plaster has crumbled and fallen away from the wall over an extensive area, revealing layers of uncoloured mortar and, below that, thin red brick. An electric junction box and a mess of wires are exposed to the elements on the corner of the building, with one wire looping up the rain gutter and disappearing off on to the roof. The side of the building possesses an astonishingly rich texture and a constant variation in colour through all shades of yellow into grimy grey and something close to black. It is decorated with a 20-foot splatter of pigeon droppings, broken metal brackets, air vents, bulges, dents, scars and pockmarks of all possible shapes and sizes.

The decomposing physical texture of the Florentine past here reminds me of the theory regarding *strati,* layers, of historical reality, as set out by Andrea Tacossa, who taught in Florence in the 1970s. He said that it was quite possible to treat, for instance, three different periods in the history of a city as distinct entities in themselves, with their own rules, characters and themes. However, since these three *strati* in fact all concerned the same place, they were bound to be heavily interconnected. Their respective realities "bled into" each other in different ways, explained Tacossa. There was the obvious "forward" bleeding, in which the realities of the city's past affected the realities of later periods. But there was also a "backwards" bleeding, where the realities, attitudes and requirements of later periods affected the interpretation and presentation of the "reality" of the past.

Ultimately any historical account is an artifice of some sort, as even the act of selecting incidents, personalities or themes for inclusion in this account amounts to a manipulation. Tacossa insisted that this did not mean there was, in fact, no objective truth regarding the history of the city, just that it was totally impossible ever to represent this. The best way of at least pointing to the existence of this elusive objective truth was to present the *strati* of history in such a way that it became clear they were not objectively true, and in fact bled into each others' "realities" in the ways he described. This would mean initially presenting to the reader the three periods of a city's history as being completely distinct but then, in the course of the historical study, gradually undermining that sense of distinctness by showing the bleeding effect in operation, both forwards and backwards. The end result would be the demolition of any sense of reality in the text, but, Tacossa argued, the realisation in the student's mind that behind all the layers and inter-bleeding there was an objective reality which could never be fully revealed to the necessarily limited gaze of the human mind.

Tacossa suggested that the same approach could also be applied to other fields, such as creative writing. A series of apparently self-contained and authentic *strati* could be fabricated and then deliberately undermined, allowing the resulting fictional reality-void to highlight the underlying intangible presence of an objective truth beyond all possible description.

* * *

The facade of *San Miniato al Monte* is of green and white marble and alongside the rectangles, triangles and a cross-within-a-circle-within-a-square is some intricate knotwork that puts me in mind of both Pictish and Islamic art. The only other colour is the blaze of gold behind a depiction of Jesus, high up on the front of the church. Inside the entrance is the "carpet of marble", famous for its fabulous arabesques, and one section is devoted to the Zodiac, the astrological signs set in a circle around the sun – the One, the centre of all reality whose light is the living energy behind all the other archetypes of our existence.

STRATO STORICO

II

Florence in 1459 was a Republic, which is to say there was no king. However, the idea that the city was some kind of democracy was, as is so often the case, very much an illusion. The place was really run by Cosimo Medici, the 70-year-old head of the family of merchants and bankers that had successfully pushed all its rivals aside to secure control over the city. The previous year Cosimo, now frequently bedridden and in pain, had withdrawn from any official public role in the administration of Florence, but his influence behind the scenes had only strengthened. He was the Godfather of the Republic, who pulled all the strings.

Medici influence spread far beyond the one city. Its financial empire, using the innovative double-entry bookkeeping system, had branches not just in Rome, Venice, Milan and Pisa but also in Geneva, Avignon, Bruges and London. While charging interest on loans was usury and not allowed, their system of foreign currency exchange managed to extract what were essentially interest charges by a cunning back-door method.

Since the Medici were officially not usurers, there was nothing in the way of a close relationship with the Vatican and they had become widely known as "God's bankers". Earlier in 1459, when Pope Pius II had headed from Rome to Mantua to declare a crusade against the Ottomans, he had stopped off in Florence on the way and had been richly entertained by Cosimo. The Pope noted in his memoirs that Cosimo "was considered the arbiter of war and peace, the regulator of law; less a citizen than master of his city. Political councils were held in his home; the magistrates he chose were elected; he was king in all but name and legal status... Some asserted that his tyranny was intolerable".[1]

But there was another side to Cosimo as well. Not content with being important and wealthy, he also wanted to be known as benevolent and wise. Thus it was that he used his banking profits to support the artists Fra Angelico and Fra Filippo Lippi, the sculptor Donatello and the architect Brunelleschi, the creator of the fabulous dome. Part of this was just vanity – the desire to be *seen to be* a patron of culture – but part of it may also have come from within. If we give him the benefit of doubt, we may imagine that he genuinely felt an inner need to balance out the crudity of gold and power with an involvement in the deeper side of life. Cosimo was certainly fascinated by magic, astrology, hermetic wisdom and ancient philosophy and gathered around him a circle of intellectuals intent on reintroducing these ideas into western European culture, without incurring risky accusations of paganism and heresy from Rome.

During the Council of Florence of 1438-39, which was an attempt to heal the East-West rift in the Christian church, Cosimo had met Gemistus Pletho, a philosopher who was to have an enormous influence on him.

Born in Istanbul/Constantinople around 1355, Gemistus had studied as a young man in Edirne, previously known as Adrianopolis, which was already at this stage under Muslim Ottoman control and which Sultan Murad I had turned into a centre of learning modelled on the caliphates of Cairo and Baghdad. Later he settled in Mystras in Greece.

In common with many philosophers of the Islamic world in which he had studied, Gemistus was a great admirer of Plato and altered his own name in homage to his hero. Although he lived in a Christian empire, Gemistus' ideas had little to do with mainstream versions of the religion. Writings such as *Summary of the Doctrines of Zoroaster and Plato* confirmed his tendency towards a much broader outlook. He suggested that behind all authentic metaphysical thought, whether manifested in the works of Hermes, Zoroaster or Plotinus, there was a *catena aurea*, a golden chain of eternal wisdom which transcended all creeds and individuals.

His social views were not entirely those of the Christian hierarchies either – he believed land should be shared rather than individually owned, for example – but despite all of this, his reputation for wisdom was so great that he had been chosen to accompany Emperor John VIII to Florence for the discussions on a union of the Orthodox and Catholic churches. While in Florence, he had lectured on the differences in Plato and Aristotle's conceptions of divinity and had written a book on the subject called *De Differentiis*, for which he was to be condemned for heresy. Greek philosophy had largely been lost to western Europe at the time – many texts had only survived thanks to the scholars of the Muslim world – and Gemistus has been credited with its reintroduction. His metaphysics so fascinated the intelligentsia of Florence that he was named "the second Plato"[2] and his injection of a distinctly Eastern-influenced Neoplatonism into Florentine culture was an essential ingredient of the *Rinascimento* thinking that was to spread from there across Europe.

While Gemistus had returned to Greece, where he had died in 1452, his influence remained very present in Florence, as did his fellow Neoplatonist Argyropoulos. Having come to Italy, like Gemistus, for the Council of Florence, the latter had been invited back by Cosimo in 1456 and had promptly been set up as Professor of Greek at the university.

Gemistus had inspired Cosimo with the dream of setting up a Platonic Academy in Florence. By 1459 an early version, with no fixed premises, had already existed for five years and among its activities was the marking of the classical philosopher's birth and death each year. The official date of this celebration was November 7 and so when, on that very day, Cosimo heard rumours of an unknown stranger expounding esoteric philosophy in the streets of Florence, his interest was particularly sparked and he sent word to Argyropoulos to see if he had any more information. We have no details of their conversation, but the professor evidently spoke encouragingly of the newcomer, for all his reservations, as word was sent to Cellini that the stranger was invited to the grand banquet in honour of Plato at the near-completed *Palazzo Medici* that very evening.

Despite the fakir's apparent distaste at the idea of mingling with the wealthy classes of Florence, Cellini does not report having had any difficulty in persuading him to accept the invitation. Perhaps the speed at which he had come to the attention of the *de facto* ruler of the Republic had suggested to him that the wheels of destiny were spinning in anticipation of a significant development in his life.

We do not know if Cellini and his family offered him a change of clothes for his appearance at this gathering of the Platonic elite, but we do know that when he turned up he was still dressed in the rough woollen tunic in which he had entered the city – according to a silk merchant present, Rinuccini, he looked like "a wild man of the unknown forests, a heathen ascetic from the wilderness beyond the walls of

Christendom".[3]

Cosimo had him seated in a place of honour – close to him, in other words! – and was seen to be in deep conversation with him throughout the meal. Rinuccini later wrote to his brother that the stranger ate hardly anything during the evening, though he was surprised to note that this "ascetic" did help himself to a reasonable amount of red wine.

When the meal was finished, and the formal toasts and readings from Plato had been carried out, Cosimo asked his new guest publicly about some of his philosophy. The merchant related that the stranger "poured scorn upon the value of wealth and status, reminding all present that life is but a temporary state of affairs and the great leveller is only but a breath away from destroying our fondest illusions" and commented, in somewhat scandalised tones, that his words "drifted far from the respected and well-ordered Platonic philosophy towards a disordered and antagonistic state of mind that ridiculed the achievements, legitimacy and moral rectitude of our host himself, not to mention those he had invited to participate in a pleasant evening of celebration".[4] But if Rinuccini expected Cosimo to also be offended, he had clearly not understood the way the Godfather's mind worked. As he reached the end of his life, the patriarch found it comforting, rather than alarming, to reflect that material success was ultimately hollow, and by internally following a spiritual path that rejected the value of the wealth and power he had amassed, he aspired to notch up a sense of achievement that would not be cancelled out by the unavoidable awareness of his own mortality.

After a while, Cosimo "leant back in his chair with a peculiar smile on his face"[5] and took out a golden florin from his money bag, showing each face of the coin to the stranger and the assembled company. On one side was the *fleur-de-lis* emblem of the city and on the other an image of John the Baptist wearing his rough hair shirt. Cosimo said that the first side represented the prestige and reputation of Florence, while the second represented its holy nature. He explained that while the two sides formed part of the same coin, it was impossible to see them both at the same time and asked the newcomer how he would resolve this difficulty. Evidently Rinuccini did not appreciate the subtlety of this question, which referred to Cosimo's difficulty in reconciling the two sides of his personality, and dismissively refers to his host having presented the preacher with "a rather pointless physical puzzle".

The stranger responded that the question had a deeper significance than his host perhaps realised, for it touched upon the essentially dual aspect of human existence – at one and the same time we are both mere flesh aspiring upwards to divine purity and divine purity yearning downwards for the fleshly incarnation that enables it to act out its will on earth.

He then took the coin and set it spinning on the tabletop. Both sides, he explained were "visible and yet invisible" in the resulting blur, the specifics of their separate natures being lost in the "great rotation of all things".

In his letter, Rinuccini writes: "I was frankly disappointed. Instead of a pearl of wisdom we had been insulted with a cheap conjurer's trick straight from the market place. I held my tongue, but somehow the trickster must have divined my disdain, for he suddenly turned and looked me straight in the eyes, with such a look as would burn a hole straight through the heart of the strongest and bravest man. I tell you, Giuseppe, there is nothing holy about this dubious individual – I swear that it is the devil himself that hides within him and he would rase Florence to the ground and drag us all off with him to his rotating hell if he were given half a chance!"[6]

Cosimo, however, was delighted with the demonstration and conclusion and warmly embraced the stranger when he left the celebration. Privately, he expressed his satisfaction at having encountered a distinctly Eastern form of mysticism.[7] He began to refer to the newcomer as "*il fachiro*", the fakir – and it was by this name that the preacher now became generally known.

The Platonic banquet marked the arrival of *il fachiro* on the Florentine scene in a truly emphatic manner. Over the next year and a half his name would be on the lips of every citizen, his words ringing in the ears of rich and poor alike, his reputation the subject of discussion around every dinner table in the Tuscan city.

And yet the working of Fate are mysterious. For today, more than five centuries later, the stranger is almost as unknown to the people of Florence as he was the day he arrived. His intrusion into the story of their city is considered inconvenient, indecent, irrelevant to the direction in which this real-life narrative subsequently veered off. Apart from the odd reference in specialist books and archived papers, his role goes unremarked and uncelebrated. It is as if the possibilities he presented during his years in Florence have been retrospectively wiped from the pages of history, the powerfully subversive aspirations that he imported and embodied deemed not to have made their way there. So complete is the denial of the significance of this remarkable man and his compelling thoughts and deeds that one would almost imagine that he had never even existed.

1. J. Najemy, *Storia di Firenze*, 2014.
2. *Storia sociale e culturale d'Italia: la cultura filosofica e scientifica*, ed. by G. Ceriotti, 1988.
3. B. Valero, *L'Arte della Seta di Firenze*, 1971.
4. Ibid.
5. Ibid.
6. Ibid.
7. M. Vecino, *Il Rinascimento e l'apocalisse*, 1954.

STRATO CONTEMPORANEO

3

I awake this morning to a terrible sense of dark foreboding. For a moment I have no idea at all as to what might have caused this, until gradually I remember the dream from which I have just emerged. I was in my room, working on the translation, when I became aware that there was someone in the stairwell outside the flat who had come to visit me, but who represented some kind of grave threat. As I emerged into the hallway I saw that my host, the lady of the house, was about to open the door to this unknown person. I tried to call out to her not to do so, but I seemed to have lost my voice and I was able to utter nothing other than a hoarse whisper that she could not have heard. As she unlocked the door and it swung open, I must have woken up, for I did not get a glimpse of whoever it was outside.

In order to shake off this unpleasant start to the day, I head straight off into the Florentine sunshine and soon find myself happily sitting by the river Arno with a Sunday morning espresso, at one of 30 or so plastic tables lined up on a gravelled area on the bank and served from a kiosk. There are further tables in a covered area and more are grouped in front of an outdoor projector screen and satellite dish.

In front of me the trees on the opposite bank are reflected in the still water. To the left, a canoe heading down the river pulls behind it a blinding silver trail of iridescence that has somehow broken free from the sun climbing over the Tuscan hills beyond.

To the right a huddle of cyclists crosses the road bridge, while in the other direction comes an excited group of youngsters dressed in the pink t-shirt uniform of a big charity run that's about to take place in the city.

Past that, along the river, is the tower of the *Porta San Niccolò* and higher up I can see the balustraded panoramic terrace of the *Piazzale Michelangelo*.

There is a fluttering beside me and I look down to see a pigeon pecking at the gravel. As he walks past my table towards the sun, the shimmering green of his neck becomes purple.

The canoe has now nearly reached the bridge and its wake gently distorts the mirror-surface of the water. The reflected rigidity of a lamp-post on the bridge is transformed into a frantically spiralling serpent before quietening into a vertical read-out from a heart monitor which is tracking the gentle demise of an exhausted existence. But before the point of death is finally reached, the canoe comes back under the bridge in the other direction and life is restored in another orgasm of joyous oscillation.

* * *

It is in the *San Marco* church to the north of the inner city centre that the feeling first gets hold of me. I am only there in the first place because I need to get my timing right for the *Accademia*, just down *Via Ricasoli*. It's a free Sunday for all the museums, which makes it a good time to visit as many as possible. But also a bad time, as everyone else has had the same idea. I've been advised to hold back until 6pm, 20 minutes before they close the doors to new visitors. That will still apparently leave me adequate time to look around before everyone is thrown out. I thought I might slip in a bit earlier than that, but the queue was still backed up right down towards *Via Degli Alfani* so I've come here instead. I am already greatly impressed by the artwork, even though the more celebrated part of the complex is shut today.

Then the organ starts up. I pay little attention at first and it acts merely as a restful backdrop to my viewing of the panels and paintings. But soon it reaches out and forces me to listen. I have no idea what the music is – it sounds ancient and somehow modern at the same time. Deep descending chords vibrate through the gold leaf of the visual splendour and fill me with what might once have been called awe. After a lifetime of indifference and, frankly, hostility to the Christian religion, I now feel moved almost to tears by this combination of powerful stimuli which speak, wordlessly, of a higher realm of being, a rarefied and beautiful mode of existence into which I could be lifted, it would seem, by surrendering myself to the glory of the Church.

I become aware that time has passed and I should now be heading for the *Accademia*, but I don't want to shake free of this spiritual intoxication. Why go to a museum, a dead collection of artworks ripped out of their intended context, when I could stay here in my *San Marco* trance, contemplating a parallel world in which I am no longer a free-thinker and an atheist but someone able to plunge himself into an unquestioning belief in Jesus Christ and his Father?

The organ piece ends and I pull myself out of the door and down the road. The delay has paid off – just three or four people left in the queue. Even though it's free to get in, I still have to be handed a ticket, which is then gravely taken off me again four steps later, leaving me with only the ripped-off counterfoil as a souvenir.

When I see Michelangelo's *David* at the end of the first hall, and the crowds of people gawping up at it, I feel like some sort of cheapskate for having managed to get up close to one of the wonders of the world of art without having either paid or queued. His *Prisoners* aren't bad, either. But for me the magic of the *Accademia* lies elsewhere, in the 13th, 14th and 15th century work that spills out from the main gallery into a special exhibition I didn't know was on and which leads me round and round and on upstairs in a daze of admiration that can only be a continuation of my experience in the church. It is strange that I can be so deeply affected by art which is devoted to figures – Jesus, Mary and various saints – who mean nothing to me personally.

It is not the object of the artists' veneration that is important at all, but the fact that they venerate, that they reach up beyond the everyday and corporeal towards an ideal-that-surpasses-all-ideals. And they express that upwards yearning by the creation of a beauty crafted from the purity and transparency of their own hearts, channelling and shaping the gilded Goodness flowing from the living essence of the universe.

What is the point of cleverness and

perspective and attempts to reproduce the shapes of everyday reality when what you are trying to depict is abstract, ethereal, on another plane to the flesh and vegetation of the world we crawl around in? What is the point of complexity when the Truth is so simple and clear? It is by shedding all the veils of illusion that we can come close to the light of the One, by stripping art bare of the superfluous so that all that is left is clarity.

As I wander spellbound through the galleries of the *Accademia*, I note the names of some of the magicians who are still channelling the light of unobstructed Being to their fellow human beings, five, six, seven hundred years after they made themselves transparent so that it could shine right through them. Filippo Lippi, Pacino da Buonaguida, Matteo di Pacino, Cenni di Francesco, Giovanni da Milano, Nardo di Cione, Orcagna, Nikolaos Ritzos, Lorenzo Monaco and all the other alchemists, named and unnamed, of the *Quattrocento* illumination – through your work you have become as eternal as any mortal being could ever hope to be.

* * *

The Medici Chapel is full of gifts from the family to the city of Florence. At least, that's what they said they were. But I have the feeling that they were gifts to themselves as much as anything – gifts that simultaneously confirmed their emperor-like wealth and status and made a gesture of atonement for it on a sufficient scale to keep their own guilty consciences at bay. Cosimo's death mask shows him, of course, with his eyes shut. This would maybe have been appropriate even when he was still alive. His eyes may have been open in their outward direction, to the Florentine world that he so dominated, but they were firmly closed to the realities of his own inner existence, no matter how he tried to hide that fact from himself by immersing himself in a banker-friendly version of Neoplatonist mysticism.

* * *

I go to make my usual breakfast this morning, only to discover that the only bread that's left is rock solid and distinctly unappetising. So I decide, as a treat to myself, to pop down to the nearest *pasticceria* and buy something there. The closest one is very close indeed – just round the corner. In fact, I am sure I recognise one of the staff. I think this place must back on to the courtyard area beneath our kitchen balcony and this woman is one of the people I have watched taking a cigarette break far below in the jumbled "canyon" between the blocks of buildings.

There is a perplexing array of pastries on offer, covered in chocolate decorations and stuffed with a range of different kinds of cream and paste. I choose one at random and the woman presents it to me in a paper napkin. I know that it's usual to order a coffee along with it, but since I can have that for free upstairs, I don't bother. Instead, once I have paid, I sit rather awkwardly at a small table in the shop eating my pastry and trying not to get too much cream over my face. They are so smart, these places. It looks more like the inside of a jeweller's than a cake shop.

I finish my sugary treat and walk the 20-odd yards back to the flat to drink coffee and start work. That wasn't the healthiest of morning outings!

The Sculptor's Hands

Once upon a time, in the great trading city of Nouruthos in the Province of Tacossa, there lived a stone mason by the name of Durro who had taken up sculpture. At first he did so merely for his own amusement, and to make gifts for his family and his friends, but gradually word of his prowess spread far afield.

His creations were amazingly lifelike depictions of the human body, in all kinds of poses and engaged in all kinds of activities. Virile young warriors brandishing spears, discus-throwers, lounging lovers, voluptuous women with swelling breasts so lovingly fashioned that one felt they must surely be tender to the touch.

The merchants, and the merchants'

wives, could not get enough of Durro's sculptures. They queued up to commission his work and to put it proudly on display outside their homes, or in the courtyards where it could be admired by guests who had been invited to dine with them with that very idea in mind, and who would go away with the determination to own one of these marvellous works for themselves.

At the same time as Durro's coffers became swollen with money, so did his head become swollen with all the compliments he received and he strayed far from the humility which had always directed his days. There were no more presents for his family and friends – and there was no time to spend with them either, for in his leisure hours he frequented the company of those who bought his work, relishing all the recognition and preening himself at their praise.

But it was not just Durro himself who was led down the path of vanity by the adulation heaped on his works. His hands, too, noticed how frequently people declared "what marvellous hands he has!" and they became proud of the part they played in the process and, increasingly, resentful towards the sculptor.

"It's all very well for him," they said to

each other while he wasn't listening. "We do all the work and he takes all the credit! And even though other people are always mentioning our skill, how often does he have the honesty and the modesty to admit that it's not him that makes the sculptures at all, but us? Never!"

The two hands pumped themselves up with self-righteous indignation at how they had been treated, until the point came when they decided to go it alone.

They simply stopped taking any notice of what Durro wanted them to do and set about making the sculptures that they themselves wanted to make.

To start with, the sculptor was not entirely sure what was happening. He could feel his hands working without his conscious involvement, but thought that this was just some new level of artistic inspiration that he had harnessed.

But when his hands started turning out sculptures that he really did not desire to make, he realised that something was going seriously wrong.

The hands were only interested in sculpting hands. In addition to their natural passion for this subject matter, they also felt, with a certain cunningness, that this would draw attention to the real creators of the sculptor's work – themselves!

Their sculptures possessed all the same beauty and diversity as Durro's previous work. There were hands holding swords, hands holding candlesticks, hands holding other hands. There were big masculine hands, slender artistic hands, sensitive womanly hands and tiny children's hands.

When his clients saw the new line of products, at first they were enchanted and declared Durro a genius for having focused on such an expressive and undervalued part of the human body.

But the interest was very much in terms of novelty, and once they had bought and displayed one of the new hand-sculptures, they were never inclined to buy a second.

Business started drying up. The sculptor gained a reputation for being an eccentric, a has-been, someone who had fallen victim to artistic dementia.

It is true that the experience was certainly taking its toll on his state of mind. He just could not understand how it was that he had lost control of his own hands.

When it came to everyday matters, they obeyed his orders. They broke bread, cut meat, held a quill, opened doors, pulled on his clothes, splashed water on his face and so on. But the moment that they picked up a hammer and a chisel they took on a will of their own and refused to take any notice of what he wanted them to do.

How he tried to make them obey! What a sight he would have made if anyone had ventured into his workshop while he was battling with them. He gritted his teeth, muttered under his breath, strained his muscles and distorted his face into an angry grimace as he attempted to direct his hands where he wished.

But still they kept filling Durro's store rooms with piles of sculptures that nobody wanted to buy. They broadened the scope of their endeavours to explore the form of the hand in more detail, making marvellously detailed thumbs, fingers and nails – all as big as the human figures that the sculptor used to make.

Then one day the sculptor, who had again been reduced to tears by his hands' wilful disobedience, was sitting in a coffee house just off the Circle of Unity in the centre of Nouruthos and overheard an intriguing snatch of conversation.

It seemed that a well-known travelling wise man, a certain Perantulo, was passing through the city and its citizens had been clamouring for his advice on all manner of conflicts, controversies and conundrums.

Durro resolved to seek out this Perantulo and ask him how he might bring his hands, and thus his work, back under his own control and, by stopping to ask everyone that he passed in the streets and alleyways of the old city, he found his way to the inn where the sage was staying.

The landlady of the place told him that Perantulo was upstairs and was not to be disturbed. Too many people had come seeking his advice while he was sitting in the public area, and he had been forced to take his flask of red wine and retreat to his room.

But Durro was not to be disparaged that readily. He went out on to the narrow flight of steps below the door of the inn and called up towards where he imagined the traveller's lodgings must be.

"O Perantulo!" he called. "I know that you are a much-sought-after man who surely deserves a rest from the clamouring of my fellow citizens, but I have a very important and unusual matter on which I wish to consult you!"

There was no response from the wall of small shuttered windows above.

"O Perantulo!" he cried again. "I appreciate that you cannot have the time to address every single problem affecting the entire city of Nouruthos, but I need your help as I have been rejected and betrayed by the two individuals who mean more to me than any others in the world!"

A window was flung open seven or eight storeys up and a woman's voice screeched at him to fasten his tongue and be gone.

But Durro persisted. "O Perantulo!" he called for the third time. "My case is stranger than you might think for these individuals are neither my friends, my parents, nor my siblings – but my own two hands!"

This time a window opened just above Durro's head and the face of an old bearded man emerged. It was Perantulo.

"What did you say?" he asked. "Your hands have betrayed you?"

"Yes, O Perantulo!" said Durro, removing his cap and bowing slightly as he spoke. "I am a sculptor by trade and yet I can no longer sculpt because these two disobedient fellows have stolen from me the direction of my work! They refuse to make what I want them to make!"

There was a long moment of silence as Perantulo looked at Durro and digested his words. And then the wise man laughed, with a laughter so infectious that all the other windows in the alleyway now flew open with sounds of merriment and there began a wave of hilarity that swept off through the narrow cobbled lanes of the city, carrying away people who could have no idea as to what had prompted it all.

Durro was invited up to Perantulo's chamber and there he explained to him everything that had been going on.

When he had finished his account, Perantulo said to him: "If I have understood you well, Durro, the sculptures you used to make yourself were mostly celebrations of the human form, is that so?"

"Yes indeed," replied Durro. "Entirely so, in fact. The human shape is my sole artistic passion."

"Your hands have learnt well from their master," chuckled Perantulo, almost under his breath. And then he looked up and asked Durro: "Tell me, if you were to regain the ability to create whatever you wanted in the way of sculptures, what would now be your inspiration?"

Durro froze with trepidation. He wanted to admit that he would still be inspired by the human form, but had the strong impression that this was not the answer the wise man was looking for. However, he could not imagine any other interesting subject matter for a sculptor, so he said nothing.

"Well," said Perantulo, after a while. "What is your answer?"

"I... I don't know!" he stammered in a thin voice.

Perantulo roared with laughter. His laughter was so infectious that the window of his room rattled in amusement, the red wine sloshed about chortling in its jar and the mice in the skirting board got a serious fit of the giggles.

"In that case, Durro, we had might as well leave your sculptures in their current hands, as at least those two errant servants have some idea as to what they are doing! Go away and think about it, O Sculptor, and, when you have an answer, come to find me and we will see if we can find a way of restoring your manual power. Good night!"

And Perantulo took a healthy swig of wine as a shame-faced Durro crept quietly out of the building and disappeared into the Nouruthossian night.

The sculptor never did return to see Perantulo and the philosopher soon moved on from the inn, from the city, from the Province of Tacossa and from that whole area of the Central World. He visited hundreds of towns and cities, met thousands of people, spoke a million words and the tale of the sculptor's hands slipped further and further back into the recesses of his mind.

Eventually, though, Perantulo's perambulations brought him back to Tacossa and to the mountains above the great city of Nouruthos, where he decided to spend the night at a renowned monastery high up in an austere and isolated fir forest.

Perantulo had in fact called there when he last blessed Nouruthos with his presence and he was pleased to recognise the same tranquil atmosphere of deepest contemplation as he pushed open the heavy wrought-iron gates and stepped inside the cloister.

But immediately he noticed something that had changed since his previous visit. The courtyard was filled with sculptures. Dozens of them.

They depicted human figures in a great number of poses and engaged in a variety of activities. Peasants holding hoes and tilling fields, women bearing jugs of water, a small boy climbing a tree to pluck a ripe apple from its boughs, a mythical hero slaying a sea-creature, a grieving father mourning the loss of his children, a holy man sitting in silent contemplation beneath an olive tree.

Perantulo was intrigued to find that the people they depicted were not perfect, but that this in some peculiar way lent the figures a positive perfection. Beyond their creased faces, bent backs and gnarled feet lay an intangible radiance. There was a clarity and purity in the form of these people that seemed to have come from far, far, away. They were filled with a grace that made their superficial flaws irrelevant to all those who beheld them.

Perantulo peered attentively at the sculpture of a crippled beggar, holding out a bowl for alms while leaning heavily on a crutch, and marvelled at the beauty that shone forth through the curves of his ears, the furrows on his brow and, more than anything, through his hands.

At this moment Perantulo suddenly stood up straight with a thoughtful expression on his face and headed off to find someone who could point him towards the creator of these sculptures.

This turned out, of course, to be Durro, who was clad in the simple attire of a Black Monk and appeared both honoured and embarrassed when Perantulo approached him and commented favourably on his art.

"Tell me, Brother Durro," asked the wise wanderer. "How was it then that you overcame the disobedience of your hands and how is it that you have forsaken your workshop to continue your work amidst the Fraternity of the One?"

"Well, Perantulo," replied the artist. "It was like this. I am ashamed to admit it, but I was mightily confused by what you asked me, and went home that evening with a muddled head and in a state of some distress.

"But the next morning I felt able to think about the situation. Not at all about what I wanted to create in the way of sculptures, as you had asked me to, but about the causes behind my hands' rebellion.

"I realised that it was nothing other than my own arrogance that had led to my downfall. There was too much of myself getting in the way of the creative spirit. I was too attached to the idea that this was my work, my talent, my means of expressing myself. I was thus not allowing the flow of creation to take its natural course. I had blinded myself to the fact that this flow came to me from the *spiritus mundi* and at the same time I had blinded myself to the fact that it found its physical expression through my hands.

"My craving to be praised for something which was not fully mine eventually became entangled with the desire for fame, for social prestige and for wealth.

"I decided therefore to take myself out of the creative process entirely, except in the sense that I acted as a channel, a connection between the idea that subsists in the ether and the action of my hands on the stone.

"I realised there could be no better place to attain that exalted state of being than here among the Black Brethren and so I immediately sold my home – the very next day after we met, Perantulo – and gave the proceeds to the monastery so that I might live out my life here".

"And your hands, Brother Durro?"

The sculptor smiled. "My hands are my hands. Ultimately they, too, are but limbs of the Whole. But they also belong to the physical presence that is me and so when I lost my obsession with the self, so did they. They still take a particular delight in shaping the hands of these sculptures, but then that is in accordance with their nature as hands. As a human being I also take a delight in reproducing variations of the form that I have assumed and this is also as it should be.

"But one thing that pleases me greatly is that when my Brothers here look at the sculptures they see beyond their form to the presence within. And nobody now speaks of the skill in my hands but of the light in my soul".

Perantulo nodded. "And tell me, Brother Durro, how is it that you did not come to tell me of your reflection and your decision, since I was still in Nouruthos at that time and would have been eager to have learnt of your experience?"

Durro shifted awkwardly from one foot to the other. "Well, Perantulo, I do not wish to cause any offence to someone so renowned as you for their sagacity and kindness, but... but..."

Perantulo raised a single eyebrow in interrogation.

"You told me to come back to you with an answer so that you could provide a solution to my problem, Perantulo. But in the end, O Wise One, I worked it out for myself. I did not need your help!"

Perantulo burst out laughing and his laughter was so infectious that the doves nestling above the cloisters, the deer in the great forest and even the trees themselves all joined in the jocularity and shook with life-affirming good humour.

STRATO STORICO

III

Who exactly was *il fachiro*? There is no record of him being known by any other name during his stay in Florence, although Vecino notes one passing reference to him as "Giovanni", which may have been made in error. Whenever he was asked, it seems that he replied by declaring his name was *Nessuno* – Nobody.

It has recently come to light that the preacher was investigated by a group of heresy-hunting clerics at the Vatican who constituted a less formal prototype of the later Roman Inquisition.[1] He is identified in one surviving document as Boulos Enducce, originally a member of an Alevi community in Transoxiana, an area of Central Asia known to the Arab world as Mawarannahr, but there is no evidence to back this up.

It certainly seems likely that his origins were to the east of Constantinople, with various rumours circulating in Florence at the time labelling him with Turkish, Armenian, Persian, Indian and even Chinese origins, though the latter claim seems unlikely to put it mildly. In stark contrast, one London merchant visiting the city at the time claimed to have recognised him as a disguised fugitive ringleader of Jack Cade's failed revolt against the English state in 1450. This surprising conclusion seems to have been drawn from the combination of "levelling and magick" that the visitor encountered in the fakir's preaching and which he mistakenly imagined to be unique to the Cade rebels he had encountered at home.[2] Confirmed descriptions of the fakir's dark-skinned appearance, along with his attested presence in Constantinople at least two years before its fall in 1453, mean we can fairly safely reject any suggestion of an English connection. We might also look to the account[3] that the fakir once said the *Duomo* in Florence reminded him of *The Dome of Soltaniyeh* in what is modern-day Iran, suggesting he had at least travelled in that part of the world, even if his origins lay elsewhere.

As far as the fakir's purpose in visiting Tuscany was concerned, we can only assume that it was chance that brought him there – or that, in the terms of the mystic mind, he was simply *meant* to be in Florence at that point in history. He clearly arrived there with a well-developed philosophy in his mind – whether this was largely personal or the reflection of a particular education we cannot tell – and was prepared to try to put it into practice in whatever situation he happened to find himself. He was a mendicant, shunning the stability of home and possessions for the greater purpose of carrying out what he regarded as his lifetime's duty.

Mendicants generally live on charity and to some extent that must have been the case with the fakir, as there is no record of him having any money to speak of. However, we do know from Cellini's account that he was happy to make himself useful on a domestic basis, spending the whole of one Sunday morning sweeping his host family's house while they attended church. Later, thanks to Argyropoulos, he was able to move into a small room in the university buildings. He may well have taken part in the communal dining arrangements there, although such domestic detail has not reached down to us across the centuries.

Given the enthusiastic welcome offered by Cosimo, one might wonder whether Florence's leading citizen might not have offered *il fachiro* a place to stay. For all we know, he may well have done so, but we can imagine that it might have been an offer that the preacher would have felt obliged to turn down. To have depended so blatantly on the *largesse* of the Medici bankers would have undermined the very principles he was seeking to assert during his visit to Florence. If the aim of his life was to secure a comfortable existence, he would never have become a wandering fakir in the first place.

The principal activity carried out by the fakir was, of course, preaching. And it was in doing so that he encountered somebody who would be just as important to him as Cellini, Argyropoulos or Cosimo – and who has crucially ensured that his existence has not been completely erased from the pages of history.

Sister Sophia was one of at least 150 Benedictine nuns of Santa Caterina who were crammed into a convent to the east of the city centre beyond *Santa Croce*. Built some half-century previously, *Le Murate* owed its name, "the walled-up", to the notorious desire of this particular order to be separated from society. Even when in church, the women preferred to remain hidden from the view of other worshippers.

It is therefore not altogether clear how Sister Sophia found herself very much in public and listening to one of the fakir's speeches, but the fact remains that this was the case. And not only that, but she wrote down a version of what he said and continued to do so on the six further occasions on which she was able to hear him. It has been suggested by Vecino that, as an older woman, Sophia had earned the necessary trust to leave the usual protection of the convent in order to investigate the nature of the spiritual message being preached to the people of the city outside. One cannot help but suspect that if indeed she was carrying out an official Benedictine investigation, the motivation behind it belonged very much to her, rather than to the institution she served, for she carried out her task with a diligence that is usually born only of great enthusiasm.

The seven "sermons" that she recorded – lending a suitably Christian mask to the content

– are plainly not the result of a *verbatim* transcription of an oral delivery, even if she had been capable of such a feat several hundred years after Hellenistic "shorthand" techniques had been forgotten and a century before the modern version began to be introduced.

The style is very much of the written language, even if we can accept that the content and construction belongs to the fakir himself. In the first sermon, for instance, we hear at one point that "the rippling of reflected sunlight shimmered and eddied across his lowered face" – this is hardly a turn of phrase that we can imagine issuing from the mouth of a man addressing a crowd of labourers in a busy urban *piazza*!

But if we are forced to concede that the sermons as presented by *Suor Sophia* are romanticised versions of the fakir's actual words, this in no way detracts from their authenticity. His own teaching reflected the traditional view that the individual speaker, writer or artist is no more than a tool for the expression of truths of universal validity – their origin stemming, in contemporary Jungian terms, from the collective unconscious rather from than the individual mind. From this perspective, Sister Sophia was also playing a part in allowing these truths to take shape on the worldly plane of existence and, of course, to ensure that they were able to reach an audience far wider than the few score Florentines gathered outside *Santo Spirito* or the Cathedral.

The nature of her part in this communication was to preserve the esoteric subtleties of the fakir's preaching for the due consideration of future generations, with the papers still available for consultation in the city archives.[4] But there was another, more exoteric, aspect to the preacher's messages that would perhaps pass us by if we were to rely exclusively on her texts.

The fakir took great pains to make it clear that the stories he told were just stories. The central character, a mystic mendicant named Perantulo, is plainly a fictional figure and the places he visits are all given exotic-sounding invented names, even if occasionally one can detect a certain similarity with real places – most obviously so in the final sermon in the series! This context gives the fakir the space in which to express ideas that might otherwise be considered subversive, as do the metaphysical tones in which they are couched.

From the rather patronising viewpoint of educated 21st century sophistication, we might imagine that all this would have gone over the heads of the simple fifteenth-century working folk who turned out to listen to Perantulo and that they were merely interested in hearing a good yarn. But the evidence suggests that, although the story-telling element would naturally have helped him gain an audience, those addressed were wise to the less obvious content of his tales.

Cellini's account, as invaluably presented by Vecino, provides the perfect complement to Sister

Sophia's rendition of the sermons, focusing as it does on the response and questions from listeners to the speeches which the student himself witnessed. He was present at *Piazza Santo Spirito* while Sophia was busy scribbling down the content of the tale she called "*Il sultano e il saggio*" – *The Sultan and the Sage.*

While the ascetic condemnation of material wealth and comfort is obviously central to this story, it is fascinating to note that one member of the audience, named only as "Nuzzi" by our witness, picked out one passing detail for a question, which he framed in such a way as to maintain the whole debate purely within the realm of the fictional.

"We heard about the butchers of the city who complained that the distribution of free meat was detrimental to their interests," Nuzzi is reported to have asked. "In the view of the wise man in the story, how far away would characters such as these have been from the acquisition of True Knowledge?"

Cellini says that the fakir replied that they were surely as far away from True Knowledge as it was possible to be, since "they have not so much as considered the possibility that there might be any Truth beyond their own immediate material gain, let alone acknowledged that this Truth might be worth seeking or, even less so, formed any intention of sacrificing any of their witless individualistic greed for the pursuit of that Truth. The wise man would have regarded the butchers of this particular ancient city as lower than the beasts they slaughtered and worthy of receiving the same justice as they were accustomed to deal out to fellow creatures untainted by the guilt that stained both their aprons and their souls".

At this, there was apparently a ripple of laughter and applause in the crowd – they had fully appreciated the radical social sub-text behind the spiritual tale and this element was assuredly a significant factor in the growing numbers of people who turned up to hear his preaching.

One question that has not been satisfactorily answered by the available documentation is whether there was more to the connection between *Suor Sophia* and *il fachiro* than the mere transcribing of his sermons. It would seem strange if a woman who attended (at least) seven of his talks, and who took such pains to write them out so elegantly, had never taken the opportunity to speak to him, but then she was a nun from a very inward-looking order and had already pushed her interests beyond the usual restraints simply by attending his preaching. Neither she nor Cellini records any contact between the two and we can probably ascribe later rumours of a blasphemous illicit liaison to the concerted efforts from some quarters to blacken the reputation of the preacher and provoke retribution against him.

1. N. Kalinić, *La persecuzione della stregoneria in Italia: continuità e discontinuità dal Medioevo all'età moderna*, 2008.
2. K. Turner, *When the South Rose Up In Anger: Jack Cade's*

Popular Insurrection, 1986.

3. M. Vecino, *Il Rinascimento e l'apocalisse,* 1954.

4. *Testamento di Suor Sophia,* Archivio di Stato di Firenze.

I sit back in my chair. It is 11 o'clock or so now and the lack of morning exercise is creeping up on me and making me feel prematurely tired. I gather myself together and head out into the sunshine, without any particular ideas about where I am going.

I pass *Santa Croce* and catch a glimpse of the hillside on the far side of the Arno, which reminds me that my hosts have recommended a visit to Fort Belvedere, which is somewhere up there. It only opens infrequently, for special art exhibitions, they have told me, so I'm lucky that my stay is coinciding with a period of public access.

I cross the river by the *Ponte all Grazie* and wend my way upwards, via the steep and picturesque *Costa San Giorgio* and shortly reach the 16th century fortress, jealously protecting the wealth of the city below from theoretical attack. Its commanding military position translates, for the civilian visitor, into vertiginous views of the whole of Florence and the hills beyond. I see a plane taking off from what looks like the middle of the city but which must be, I cleverly deduce, the airport. In the far distance, the mountains are engulfed in a cloudy haze that rises into hazy cloud. Wandering around the fort you see the celebrated *Giardino di Boboli* below, and the back of the *Palazzo Pitti*. To the north is an olive orchard, cypress trees, the turret of a castle-folly and the rising of gentle hills. Further round you can see the coach-crowds gathered to enjoy the views at *Piazzale Michelangelo* and, looking over them, the beautiful *Santa Miniato al Monte*.

I wander around the terraces, enjoying the space both here and beyond. There is the phut-phutting of a sprinkler on a patch of lawn and the constant thudding of techno music issuing incongruously from the open air cafe.

The art installation turns out to be by Anthony Gormley, the English sculptor behind the *Angel of the North* in Gateshead. Part of it is ugly. Maybe on purpose, but nevertheless ugly. Shapes and figures assembled from small metal blocks, most of which are coated in rust. Scrap yard left-overs that can only have got up here by leaping from a steam-powered freight-zeppelin passing overhead on its way to the industrial dumping grounds of Africa or the Far East. But much of it has a certain elegance. Life-sized iron figures, stripped down and smoothed out to their barest level of humanity and then forcibly riveted to their mineral essence by the large squares scarring their bodies. One perches on the ramparts over the main entrance. One lies face-down on the ground, balancing only on the tip of his toes and the top of his head. Some have fallen down flights of steps. One faces a wall, head bowed. Sobbing, perhaps. Another writhes on the ground in pain, half way down a slope. The security guard below, walkie-talkie in permanent crackle-mode, pays no attention to his plight.

The centrepiece of the art installation is a row of twelve figures stretching from the centre of the main terrace towards a corner commanding unrivalled views of Florence. The first of these is crouching, the second somersaulting, the third sitting with arms on knees, the fourth has stretched out his legs, the fifth is on his haunches, the sixth is kneeling, the seventh sitting on an unseen chair, the eighth stands with lowered head, the ninth is tilting forward, the tenth leaning back, the eleventh is upright and the twelfth stands tall with head raised high. But what is he looking at? It doesn't seem to me that he is taking in the view of Florence like the rest of us. He's not gazing down at the red roofs and towers spread out below him like a Roman feast, I conclude, after carefully assessing the angles. He's looking up, at something even higher than this highest point. At this very moment, and I swear this is true, the midday bells ring out in the city below. From the *Duomo*, from the *Santa Croce*, from other churches that I cannot identify, all their patterns and pitches converging in a cacophonic collision and floating up out of the urban river valley in a great chime-cloud that reaches exactly the point at which the ironlooker is gazing so intently before gently fading and sinking and slipping back down into the solitary tolling of just one church bell.

* * *

Every evening I earn my keep by taking part in a two-hour English conversation session with my hosts. This is inevitably more stressful for them than it is for me, since I am not only able to speak my own native tongue but am also able to play the role of the expert, whose knowledge is absolutely unchallengeable by mere non-Anglophones. We wander through a variety of subjects and one evening chance upon the theme of film directors. It turns out there is a significant overlap in my taste and theirs. Ingmar Bergman, Wim Wenders, Jim Jarmusch, Krzysztof Kieślowski, Louis Malle and Werner Herzog all get a mention. But most of all we pay our respects to Andrei Tarkovsky.

The very next day I am walking back along the southern side of the river, in *Via San Niccolò*, when I discover, to my astonishment, a plaque marking a building where Tarkovsky lived for a while, just before his untimely death. It turns out he was made an honorary citizen of Florence and his son still lives here, running the *Fondazione Tarkovskij*. I later find an online interview with the son, in which he reveals that the conversation between father and boy in *The Sacrifice* was very much a message from the director to his child. I then look back at a blog post I once wrote about the film, which quotes the father's words: "Some wise man once said that sin is that which is unnecessary. If that is so, then our entire civilisation is built on sin, from beginning to end. We have acquired a dreadful disharmony, an imbalance if you will, between our material and our spiritual development. Our culture is defective, I mean our civilisation... If only someone could stop talking and *do* something instead".

STRATO STORICO

IV

It was inevitable, given the nature of his message, that the fakir would quickly attract enemies as well as admirers and the first of those on record is Girolamo Orsini, a rather peripheral member of a leading Italian aristocratic family who was involved in banking and trade.

In her 1994 book *La storia degli Orsini*, Lucia Lezzerini cites a letter from Girolamo to his cousin Napoleone, dated February 1, 1460, in which he complains of "the birth of a new spirit of discontent among the bestial classes of Florence" which was threatening the stability and prosperity of the Republic. He highlights the role of "an immigrant, a foreign agitator come to spread turmoil under the guise of religious teachings".[1] Orsini goes on to describe this unnamed man as "*un anarchico*", an anarchist, in one of the earliest recorded usages of this term, even it was intended as an insult rather than as a serious political label. At this stage, Orsini's words were little more than a grumble, but as the months went on, the dislike that many wealthy

Florentines felt towards *il fachiro* inevitably hardened into a more concrete and pro-active hostility.

One interesting and somewhat mysterious aspect of the fakir's presence in Florence is his relationship with the Neoplatonist philosopher Marsilio Ficino. When the traveller arrived in the city, Ficino was 26 years old. His father was Cosimo's personal doctor, Diotifeci d'Agnolo, a fact which had provided him with an easy route into the centre of power. Ficino was originally educated in the Aristotelian tradition, under Nicholas Tignosi, and by the time he was 21 had already written *Summa philosophiae*, a treatise in Latin inspired by the Greek masters. It has been said that the direction in which young Ficino's work was taking him alarmed the Archbishop of Florence, Antonino Pierozzi, who tried to steer him away from "Platonic heresy" by despatching him to Bologna to study medicine from 1457 to 1458,[2] but when he returned to Florence his interest in Neoplatonism seems to have been undiminished[3] and in 1459 he became a pupil of Argyropoulos, alongside Cellini. The concerns of the Church regarding the theological correctness of the great works of Greek philosophy may not have deterred Ficino from his lifetime's work of translating and analysing them, but they did undoubtedly play a role in shaping his personal version of Platonism. He veered completely away from the pagan approach of Gemistus, who had so inspired Florence with his exotic metaphysics, and instead worked to combine Platonic thought with Christianity, producing a new hybrid philosophy that would be acceptable to the religious authorities. Perhaps Ficino was shrewd enough to realise that this was necessary in the interests of self-preservation. With his continued promotion of Hermetic texts, occult ideas, alchemy and astrology,[4] he was constantly walking a thin line as far as Rome was concerned and later in life he was to come a hair's breadth from falling foul of the Inquisition, being accused of sorcery by Pope Innocent VIII in 1489.

We cannot know what was going through Ficino's head when the fakir barged into the intellectual milieu around Argyropoulos and Cosimo in which he was only just beginning to make his presence felt. A journal entry unearthed by Bernardeschi[5] from the early part of 1460 seems to refer to the preacher. Ficino wrote: "I have been reminded by recent events of the paramount importance of scholarship to the understanding and communication of the ideas which are essential to the well-being of humanity. A passionate but careless individual, who speaks from the heart without first purifying his emotions through the processes of intellect, must be regarded as dangerous. He is dangerous to society as a whole because he unleashes powerful ideas without ensuring that they are carefully contained within the necessary order of things of which they are a part and which they must serve to maintain. He is dangerous to those with whom he associates because he undermines

the seriousness of their studies and writing by
the looseness of his tongue, dragging them into
the flames of irresponsibility which are fanned by
his words. And, finally, he is dangerous to
himself for, by failing to carefully consider the
path he must take, he leaves himself open to
ambush by those whose interests have been
imperilled by his activities".

Ficino, we might assume from this, was
someone who did "carefully consider the path he
must take" and it seems that he carefully
considered that this path should avoid *il fachiro*
as far as was possible. Cellini refers in passing to
"*il geloso Marsilio*", the jealous Marsilio Ficino,
and it certainly seems feasible that Ficino might
have resented the attention attracted by *il
fachiro* that he may have felt was rightfully his,
as a rising star of Renaissance philosophy. It is
worth bearing in mind that the line about
someone leaving themselves "open to ambush by
those who have been imperilled by his activities"
could be retrospectively interpreted as a kind of
threat, even if it not openly expressed as such.

There was certainly a significant difference
between the philosophy developed by Ficino and
that voiced by the fakir, despite their apparent
common roots in Platonic, Hermetic or what
might today be termed "perennialist" thought.
This was not merely a question of detail, either,
but a divergence that can be traced back to the
very core of their respective metaphysics.

We see this clearly in the second of the two
sermons transcribed by *Suor Sophia*, entitled

The Lesson at The Tavern, where the fakir presents, via his fictional avatar, the notion that all of us are "part of what is, always has been and always will be the reality of the entire Universe".

This statement is entirely in line with the classical Neoplatonist viewpoint – it could almost be a direct quotation from Plotinus, for instance – and yet it leads towards dangerous territory for anyone trying to remain within the permitted boundaries of Christian theology. It is only a permissible position if there is added on to that idea of an all-inclusive organic universe the notion of a transcendent God, who created all of this and remains outside of it.

The fakir, through the fictional character Perantulo, never actually denies that there is a transcendent divinity, but at the same time he never states, nor even vaguely implies, that there might be one.

This leaves his position as being closer to a pantheistic conception of a living universe that is, in effect, its own god. Even with the possible addition of the idea of a transcendent level of abstraction, an idea of the Whole which is broader than the merely physical matter of the cosmos, it still does not amount to a God in the way that is, of course, essential from a Christian perspective.

The implications of this stance rippled outwards from the theoretical to the very practical. If the idea of "divinity" is ascribed to the wholeness of the universe, rather than to something outside of it, then the concept of authority is cut off at its source.

This was evidently not lost to the more attentive members of the crowd who listened to the "tavern" sermon, as Cellini relates. An unnamed woman apparently asked the fakir what Perantulo would have said if he had been asked "whether some amongst us were more important parts of the universe than others and were thus worthy of demanding obedience from their fellows".[6] *Il fachiro* replied that his fictional mage would probably have replied that "because all are One and only temporarily separate, we cannot talk in terms of parts that possess any distinct value and that any person claiming to command obedience was blaspheming against the unity of the Whole". This is a far cry from the conservative Platonic concept of an ordered hierarchy, a microcosmic human world in which all know their allotted place just as surely as the stars know their place in the heavens. We might think that the aristocratic Orsini may have inadvertently hit on exactly the right word when he condemned the fakir as an "anarchist".

1. L. Lezzerini, *La storia degli Orsini*, 1994.

2. G. Semprini, *I platonici italiani*, 1926.

3. G. Saitta, *Marsilio Ficino e la filosofia dell'umanesimo*, 1954.

4. S. Gentile, "Il ritorno di Platone, dei platonici e del 'corpus' ermetico. Filosofia, teologia e astrologia nell'opera di Marsilio Ficino", in C. Vasoli (ed.), *Le filosofie del Rinascimento*, 2002.

5. F. Bernardeschi, *Marsilio Ficino: filosofo, umanista e astrologo*, 2006.

6. M. Vecino, *Il Rinascimento e l'apocalisse*, 1954.

STRATO CONTEMPORANEO

5

While I am in the *Cappella Brancacci*, admiring the famous frescos by Masolini and Masaccio, a strange thought strikes me. All the scenes in the life of St Peter are represented in the physical setting of *Rinascimento* Florence. This looks fine now, through our eyes – a beautiful backdrop to any work of art. But how did that seem at the time? How would it look to us today if an artist depicted biblical scenes in the streets of contemporary London, New York or Frankfurt? Wouldn't we think that was a bit odd? And who are all these people in the painting, their likenesses sometimes portrayed in near-photographic detail? Do they really represent historical figures present at the time of this important episode of the Christian religion or are they cameo appearances for contemporaries of the artists, well-known characters of the 15th century scene in Florence – merchants and bankers perhaps? A message from our sponsors?

Are the frescos about Christianity at all, in fact, or is the dominant religion just a convenient vehicle for the boundless vanity of a citizenry that felt itself to be at the centre of the world and the heart of human history and was slipping rapidly away from the celebration of the spirit into the celebration of itself?

Occupying the central position between the two facing walls of the celebrated frescos is the simple gilded Byzantine glory of the *Madonna del Popolo*. This 13th century work by an unknown Tuscan artist completely outshines all the clever and influential artistic innovation that surrounds it. It has meaning.

* * *

I am wandering along a long, narrow, slightly uninteresting road just east of the city centre behind two young men, possibly students, engaged in animated conversation. Suddenly, they turn off through a small archway and I decide, impulsively, to go the same way and find out if there is anything to see down there. After a few paces, I nearly turn back. It seems to be just a block of flats. But I keep following them and we come out in a courtyard which is clearly a public space. There are trees, benches and, on the far side, a restaurant and some public toilets.

I sit in the shade under a tree and look

around a bit more carefully. The walls of the buildings surrounding the courtyard are high and obviously old, but the whole place has recently been refurbished. Many of the windows now open out on to modern metal balconies brimming over with pot plants and vines, though others are criss-crossed with metal bars. In the centre of the yard three boys, aged eight or nine, are playing around a constantly-flowing drinking-water fountain. A couple of pigeons preen themselves and then flap off to the opposite corner. The air is filled with a general lunchtime clinking of cutlery, not only from the restaurant but from the open windows of the unseen flats all around me. Occasional snatches of conversation are blown out into the courtyard and drift down to where I am sitting.

A bright green plastic ball rolls past my bench, duly followed by a three-year-old girl in a white summer dress. She fetches the ball, then runs and throws it at her mother, or perhaps grandmother, who – while continuing to munch contentedly on an apple – traps the ball with her foot with near-professional expertise and sends it skimming back off again for the child to chase.

Another woman sits breastfeeding her baby under the trees near the restaurant, buggy parked up beside her.

A tiny delivery van backs in through the far entrance, the driver concentrating hard with a cigarette in his mouth as he rapidly spins the steering wheel to make a tricky turn.

A bearded individual, listening to music through headphones, comes and sits on a bench to my left and takes a piece of plastic Tupperware out of his bag.

Five men in their 40s or 50s, all in jeans and polo or t-shirts, amble slowly across the yard. The oldest of them is almost bald and what's left of his hair is grey, but he still boasts the tiniest and neatest of ponytails on the back of his head. He walks with a cowboy swagger.

I see that the breastfeeding mother has now been joined by the ball-control woman – it looks as if she is the grandmother, after all.

The bearded man's plastic tub turns out to be full of pasta, which he eats enthusiastically with a fork, while the group of middle-aged men have reached the restaurant and are looking through the menu. Their casual air gives me the impression that they generally dine out at midday and are quite satisfied that they have the money to be able to do so.

I notice that two young women who just walked into the yard have now left it through a gateway bathed in blue light refracted through a coloured plastic awning. I decide to investigate.

In a passageway there is a small bookshop and beyond lies another courtyard. Here is another refreshment outlet with the slightly ostentatious name of *Caffè Filosofico*.

This immediately strikes me as the ideal place in which to have a coffee and spend a quarter of an hour translating a few more lines of *Il fachiro* – as well as I can do with only the small Italian dictionary that I carry around with me.

Behind the counter is a slim, dark-haired woman wearing a simple black dress and a white serving apron. When she looks up to take my order, I am taken aback by her face. I wouldn't describe her as "pretty" in the conventional way. There is something far too serious about her for that and her features show the strain of four or maybe five decades of living. But, it feels to me at that moment, she is radiating a kind of gentle purity that can only come from a deeper, internal beauty. Her delicate features are lit up with the faintest of half-sad half-smiles. I feel I want to talk to her, but it doesn't feel appropriate to do any more than take my espresso and thank her.

I go back outside, choose a table as far away as possible from the young women who led me in this direction and are now chatting loudly over their drinks, and take out the book, dictionary, notebook and two pens – it's always advisable to carry two pens as one of them is always liable to give out without notice. I take a sip of coffee and look around me. Two of the walls in this yard feature barred windows – the one behind the *caffè* is particularly severe-looking and the bars are thicker. The others walls are punctuated by modern pods sticking out from the side of the building – enclosed balconies for the flats within, fitted with Venetian blinds to keep out the heat of the summer sun. At the far end of the yard is an outdoor stage, framed with lighting rigs.

I pick up *Il fachiro* and start to scribble down the next section of my English version. I leave plenty of space on the pages of the notebook as I often revisit sections and improve on the original draft. But before long, I have come across a phrase for which I cannot come up with a proper translation – *"sottigliezze filosofiche"*. I already know that *sottigliezze* means "details" and the mini-dictionary confirms this. But it just doesn't make any sense here. Philosophical details? What are they? Metaphysical facts? I could leave it for now, and carry on, but I am frustrated by the gap in my understanding. I really just want to go back to the flat and use my hosts' large dictionary or the internet to find a solution. I put the book down and gaze out across the yard, failing to notice the approach, from behind me, of the woman from inside, who has come round to clear tables. I glance round to find her right next to me. She smiles and then she catches sight of the book on the table. "Oh!" she says. "May I look?"

I say that of course she can, explaining that I

am trying to translate it into English. She lifts the book very gently, studying first the front cover and then the back, before gingerly opening it up at the point which I have marked with an old cafe receipt. "*Sottigliezze filosofiche*" she says out loud, picking out the very phrase over which I have been pondering. "How would you say that in English, I wonder? Not 'details' here, but perhaps – 'niceties'? Am I right?" I am astonished and tell her that this is the very word I have been looking for! Philosophical niceties. Of course!

I end up staying in the cafe courtyard for nearly two hours – and for three espressos. The woman – called Sofia as I now know – pops outside from time to time and comes over to see if I need any help with understanding the Italian. She is so much more useful than a search engine or a dictionary, with her excellent knowledge of English combined with explanations about the sense of the original text, and it's a delight to combine my work with the pleasure of human contact. I am flattered by her interest in my work and thrilled that she seems to share the same fascination with the book I am translating. She tells me that she's never seen it before but she's sure she's heard something about the *fachiro* himself, maybe a long time ago from her grandfather, who was a keen student of Florentine history. I offer to lend her the book if I manage to finish my task before my month here is up and she jokes that at this rate she will have read it all by then in any case, in the dribs and drabs of the passages she has been looking at with me.

Finally, I have to leave because it's time for the English conversation session with my hosts. I thank her warmly for her help and express the hope that I will see her again. She tells me that she'll be here again at the same time tomorrow.

STRATO STORICO

V

There is now indisputable evidence that the fakir's contribution to an increasing spirit of rebellion in Florence went a lot further than the preaching for which he has so far been known.

By the later months of 1460, a year after the wanderer's arrival in the city, Orsini's enmity had taken on a more definite form. While researching this book, I discovered papers in the *Archivio di Stato di Firenze* from the Orsini family estate. Amidst endless accounts and legal correspondence was filed a series of reports from what can only be professional spies hired to monitor the activities of *il fachiro*. As one might expect, they are unsigned and not specifically addressed to Orsini, although the context of their discovery leaves little doubt in this regard. They do not even refer clearly to the object of their research, referring to him instead as "Giovanni" or "G", a code word with an intriguing echo in the passing use of that name picked up by Vecino in his book. With these notable exceptions, the pages of the reports are full of detail. Although there are many gaps in the documentation which remains, the authors appear to have been providing a very complete account of the fakir's movements and connections between August and October 1460.

In short, we learn that "Giovanni" spent most of his time in the Oltrarno district across the river from the seat of power, even after he had moved into his university lodgings. Some of the detail correlates with what we already know about him – the entry relating to August 20, for example, refers to him delivering a sermon in the *Piazza di Cestello* in which he spoke of "a river bursting its banks". This is the account that Sister Sophia preserved for posterity as *Perantulo and the Water*, in which the fakir expounds a kind of 15th century existentialism when he has Perantulo declare that "the freedom to accept responsibility is the freedom to take on the burden of being". The philosophical niceties were, however, lost on the anonymous spies, who warned instead that "G may be attempting conspiracy to block River Arno, possibly by destroying Ponte Vecchio, and causing serious flood damage to city centre". This may seem a laughable interpretation of the sermon, but maybe the spies were not as stupid as their report suggests – their continued employment depended, after all, on maintaining Orsini's paranoia regarding the fakir's intentions and the threat they presented to his personal wealth and lifestyle. Since the agents were probably not capable of assessing the potential ideological impact of the fakir's presence, in which lay his true significance, they were obliged to whip up some more practical threats that might be emanating from it, so as to justify their role.

We can detect the same reasoning behind the constant references to the extra-Florentine connections of people seen to be associated with the fakir. So and so "has a brother in Naples". Someone else "is known to have lived for many years in Venice". Another person "is believed to be of French extraction and to maintain close contacts with that kingdom". None of this adds up to anything in particular, but suggests that one of the specific tasks with which these agents had been charged was to establish the preacher's link to some rival power base as a means of discrediting him. The more obvious route to this, of course, was his own foreign origin and it was this line of attack that was to be thoroughly exploited later on.

Orsini's spies had more muck-raking luck with their investigation of private gatherings attended by the fakir.

In the seven months since his arrival, he had clearly made some important contacts with the discontented classes of Florence, presumably as a result of his preaching but also perhaps stemming from his frequenting of the local taverns. He had evidently been taken into the confidence of a circle of would-be revolutionaries, who were no doubt excited by the potential of his oratory in turning a general sense of resentment towards the ruling elite into an actual insurrection along the lines of the 14th century *Tumulto dei Ciompi,* no longer in living memory but still an inspiration for sporadic outbreaks of defiance.

The spies diligently set out the addresses where these secretive meetings were held, along with those present – the names of frequent participants are reduced to initials by the time the remaining papers pick up the story. We do not now know whether the spies named themselves, or their alter egos, among the attendees – this would have been a prudent move in case of their reports falling into the hands of those who could identify them by a process of elimination! However, we can surmise that one or more of them was present at each of these meetings and was thus able to report on what was said.

The reports are the work of mercenary spies, and not of men of letters, and so do not generally make for an entertaining read, except in terms of their clumsiness and exaggeration. A general flavour may be gained by looking at the record for September 13, 1460. "G attended number 91 *via S. Niccolò*, home of A.T. Also in attendance were G.N, P.P., L.U., E.M., Guido Lanfredini, Maria Cocchi. Talk of need for self-sacrifice. Current society based on sin. G. spoke of 'disharmony and imbalance'. A.T. said people should stop talking and do something instead. Enthusiastic agreement from all present. Group clearly represents serious threat to social stability. Further surveillance strongly recommended".

It is worth noting, in passing, that those charged with following the fakir around Florence failed to make a single note, in the preserved documentation at least, of any one-to-one encounter with Sister Sophia.

STRATO CONTEMPORANEO

6

I wouldn't mind living in one of these, I find myself thinking as I peer into another of the monks' cells in the museum part of *San Marco* – the church whose organ filled me with such inspiration before my visit to the *Accademia*.

Not nowadays, of course. Not with a steady stream of people like me poking their heads through the door to have a look around – or, in the case of a woman just ahead of me, poking their camera through the door for a quick snap, without even really actually looking at what's there. A nice little study/bedroom featuring vaulted ceiling, red-tiled floor, a window set into the wall and a pair of heavy wooden shutters, studded with large metal bolts. Oh, and a Fra Angelico fresco. I like the fact that each door has a lock and a little knocker ring on the outside. The Dominican residents must have been allowed a certain amount of privacy, despite the communal nature of their existence. Every single cell has, in the same position, a unique piece of sacred art by Angelico, that winged messenger of the early Renaissance known in Italy as *il Beato Angelico*, the Blessed Angelic One. Many are crucifixion scenes, with blood dripping down from the pierced chest of the suffering Christ.

Right at the end of a row of cells I find myself in a sort of shrine to the rebel priest Girolamo Savonarola. The bust on display could be of a current-day member of the Black Bloc, one of the thousand-strong anarchists who smashed up and firebombed a small part of Milan a few months ago in a secular modern-day version of his famous "bonfire of the vanities". Within the black hood is an idealist's face, chiselled by the far-away fortitude of a visionary who would transform dreaming into deeds.

I walk back past the monks' cells, read a plaque marking the spot where Savonarola was arrested on April 8, 1498, just before his execution, and enter the monastery library, now sadly bereft of nearly all its 400 or more titles. It appears to be dedicated to the memory of two important men in the history of the Dominican order – Albertus Magnus, a 13th century friar, and his pupil, fellow Dominican priest Thomas of Aquinas. For all the saintliness of the canonised medieval pair, there are aspects of their philosophical interests that seem to stray a little beyond the narrow confines of what would today be considered the Christian faith.

Albertus, for instance, has a reputation for having been a bit of an alchemist on the quiet, and even for having passed on these secrets to Aquinas. It's not clear whether this has anything to do with Aquinas' legendary ability to levitate.

While the Church likes to dismiss the alchemy connection, there's no denying that Albertus was very much into astrology – again, not a subject now normally taught at Sunday School or frequently mentioned in the lyrics of the abysmal self-hating dirges that have so successfully repelled generations of suffering schoolchildren from the Christian faith. "O Jesus, I have promised to serve Thee to the end; Be Thou forever near me, my Master and my Friend; Especially since Mercury's about to move into Sagittarius".

Old Albert's love of astrology is even blazoned all over a piece of art which celebrates his teaching, just inside the *San Marco* library. Two little circular paintings, "medallions", depict young women representing the dual loves of his philosophical life – logic and astrology.

On the other side of the doorway, over which hangs Albertus' portrait, is a twin to the first painting – a depiction of *La Scuola di San Tommaso d'Aquino*. Sitting in front of Aquinas are three thinkers – 13th century Burgundian William of Saint-Amour, third century Libyan priest Sabellius and, in centre place, the Muslim philosopher Ibn Rushd, known in Europe as Averroes.

The Islamic connection is fascinating, especially in the light of the present-day demonisation of a culture that is in fact deeply intertwined with our own. Albertus, too, was a student of both Ibn Rushd and Persian polymath Ibn Sina, aka Avicenna, a leading light of the Islamic Golden Age whose prolific 11th century writings covered philosophy, metaphysics, medicine, mathematics, logic, astrology and, yes, alchemy. Not that Albertus would have been interested, if you accept the official line.

* * *

Perspective is a strange thing, it strikes me. If you take three parallel lines heading off into the distance they appear to converge on the horizon and that is therefore the way they are depicted in a painting representing the world as we see it. But in fact, of course, they do not converge and would theoretically continue to run parallel to each other for an infinite distance. The represented "reality" in which they converge is merely a subjective reality, seen from the perspective of one particular point of observation. The objective reality of the lines continuing to run in parallel for ever more cannot be seen or depicted by us, because we can never escape from our subjectivity. I wonder how this fits in with Tacossa's theories. For him, the merger of three layers helps reveal the existence of objective truth, whereas, in the case of perspective, the apparent convergence of the three lines surely helps to conceal its existence through the triumph of illusory subjective reality?

PERANTULO AND THE WATER

From time to time, when Perantulo was weary of the ways of men, he would retreat into the vastness of the forests or the deserts or the mountains and soak himself in soothing solitude.

However, even here his fame was great and his advice would often be sought by forms of the Oneness which seem to be invisible, irrelevant or insentient in the noisy, bustling surface-world of humankind.

One afternoon the sage was walking by the shore of an enormous lake, which had evidently swollen beyond its usual size as its waters were swilling around half-submerged shrubs, trees and grasses.

Suddenly he became aware of a particular kind of lapping sound coming from a little inlet ahead of him and, as his ears became attuned to its voice, he understood that it was speaking to him thus:

"O Perantulo, Wise Man of the Race of the Unwise, stay a moment, pray, so that I may ask of you the benefit of your understanding!"

The wanderer stopped and invited the speaker to go on.

"O Perantulo, He who Spans that which Cannot be Spanned, please listen to the doubts of a humble splash of water. As you can see, O Sage, the natural state of this lake has been disturbed. A great rockfall, aided by fallen trees and debris, has blocked the means by which we, the waters, should flow out and beyond and down to the ocean. We are trapped here and all the time we rise further and further up the shore. Eventually we must spill over the lowest point in the surrounding land and find some new route down the valleys. My fear is this, Perantulo – that I, of all splashes of water, am best placed to be the first to make this move. See how even now I creep closer to that gravel ridge, beyond which the hills slopes forever down!"

"I understand, O Water Spirit," spoke Perantulo. "But at the same time I don't.

Why is it that you fear your role in being the first to break free from these confines?"

"O Perantulo," replied the water, "we both know that the Great World Philosophy places untold importance on the togetherness of all things and on our responsibility to remain true to ourselves by remaining true to our origins. I am afraid that if I break free from the confines of these shores I will also be breaking free from the bond which is the only meaning to my existence!"

Perantulo looked at the water, which to anybody else's ears would merely have been gently lapping on the beach, and sighed. His sigh was so heavy that it blew up a great wave which surged across the surface of the lake and disappeared into the distance.

"O Witless Water," he responded at length. "Have you forgotten what the Great Philosophy teaches us? If we wish to remain true to the Whole we must remain true to ourselves. And, at the same time, if we wish to remain true to ourselves we must remain true to the Whole. To accept the responsibility of being true to the Whole is to accept the responsibility of being ourselves. Your responsibility to the Whole of the water here is to accept your individual responsibility to be the first part of it to break out of this trap. If you were to refuse to do so, despite the opportunity offered to you by Fate, then you would have failed not just yourself, but the Whole!"

When the water heard these words, it knew that Perantulo was right and it no longer held back from its duty. As Perantulo moved on up towards the mountain peaks, the water edged more and more quickly towards the ridge that was the last obstacle in the way of its freedom.

Slowly one finger reached round the last rock in its way and, all coated in dust and soil, began to trickle cautiously downhill. As the movement began, it wore away the earth beneath it, carved out a deeper and wider channel away from the lake's shore and thus allowed more water to join the rebellion.

The more the flow increased, the more capacious became the channel through which it could pass. The original rock that had blocked its path was swept away, as was the ridge itself and soon the water was flowing in torrents into the newly-formed stream.

But at the head of this flow, now far down the mountainside, the original lapping water was unhappy and was calling out to Perantulo for help.

"O Perantulo!" it shrieked up into the forest. "What has become of me? I was so pure and gentle when I sprang from the earth and when I flowed into the lake. But now my face is all covered in dirt and leaves and my back is scarred by branches and pine cones! And I am the cause of so much destruction! The movement that I have unleashed is toppling trees, flooding burrows, sweeping away nests, drowning hundreds of tiny innocent creatures who have the misfortune to find themselves in its path! I am so ashamed, Perantulo! If I could stop all this now, I would, but it is too late! How can I possibly live with myself?"

As Perantulo heard the gushing words of the water he pushed his way through the thorny trees that lined his high mountain path and found his way to a rocky outcrop from where he could look down to the slopes below and the bubbling, frothing, path being scoured through the vegetation by the new river.

And when he had taken in the message, he gave a deep sigh. It was such a sigh that a huge wind swept out across the peaks and the plains beyond, raising dust clouds in the desert and rattling the windows of the fishermen's cottages on the coast, two hundred miles away.

"O Woeful Water," he shouted eventually. "You have taken upon yourself the task of acting for the Whole of the water to which you belong and now you are filled with concerns about what you vainly regard as your individual purity! Have you remembered nothing of the wisdom of our elemental ancestors? We must do what we must do. Should a farmer be ashamed of the dirt under his fingernails? Should a carpenter be ashamed of wood shavings? Should the sun be ashamed of the shadow? The freedom to accept responsibility is the freedom to take on the burden of being in all its aspects".

The water understood that he was right and continued on its way with no more qualms, carving its way downwards with a still-increasing mass of water on its tail, while Perantulo shook his head to himself and resumed his upward path.

Before long, the natural course of the new river took it crashing out of the forest into the bed on which had originally lain before its progress had been blocked. With the first splash leading the way, it screamed with delight to find itself back on course and, as the channel leading from the lake eroded more and more of the shore and allowed more and more water to pass, the river regained its previous glory as it danced merrily down the valley.

Such was its energetic turbulence that the splash of water which had led the breakthrough quickly lost its place at the head of the procession and became an anonymous little wave in the great confusion of current.

From up high on the very summit of the tallest mountain in the range, Perantulo heard its plaintive voice call out to him. "O Perantulo!" it gurgled. "I do not understand at all what I am supposed to do now! I took on the onerous task of leading the water to liberty, bearing the burden of responsibility as you said I must, but nobody seems to care! The rest of the water keeps pushing past me, leaping over me, forcing me this way and that and none of it ever pauses to thank me, or acknowledge me or even to glance at me briefly in such a way that I know it is aware of what I have done!"

Perantulo looked up at the sky and sighed the biggest sigh yet, which sent clouds scudding away, span the moon round on her axis and scattered the stars in distant and mysterious galaxies.

"O Wearisome Water!" he bellowed from his mountain top. "You speak as if the True

Philosophy were not embedded in your very essence! The river is flowing again as it should. Nature, acting through you, has reasserted itself and all is well. There is no more need of your particular individuality or of the resolve you showed in sticking to the task in hand. If there had been no blockage, you would never have been called on to play this role, with all the anguish it has caused you. But, as it was, you played your part, did what was asked of you and fulfilled your purpose as it was unveiled to you. What greater satisfaction could there be? Be at peace, O Wondrous Water, for you have been all that you were ever meant to be".

The water knew for sure that Perantulo was right and it bubbled on in bliss towards its union with the waiting sea.

My general sense of well-being has again been tainted by a nightmare – the same one as before, in fact. Again I am working on the translation in my room, although I have the impression that maybe Sofia is there beside me. Again there is someone at the front door whom I know to be a threat to me and again I am unable to stop my hostess from letting them in. This time, however, the dream lasts long enough for me to catch sight of the figure outside. It is a very large man. I can only see him in outline but I imagine that he is some kind of riot cop, soldier or other violent thug – certainly someone who wishes me harm.

I awake with that same deep and gnawing sense of unease that I previously experienced. It takes me the best part of an hour to rid myself of the negativity and start work. While I am making a coffee I even find myself peering down over the kitchen balcony trying to work out exactly which way I would try to climb down to safety if necessary. I tell myself to snap out of it and to stop being so ridiculous. I remind myself that it was a dream rather than an actual event and that I am a relatively normal person living a relatively normal life and not a character from some absurd and melodramatic film or novel.

* * *

My visits to the courtyard have now become a part of my daily routine – at least on the days when Sofia is working. It turns out this is none other than *Le Murate,* once the home of Sister Sophia! Since her time, it has also served as a men's prison, from 1845 until 1985. Maybe there's something about this historical connection that helps to inspire me – but the translation seems to flow so much better when I am working there!

STRATO STORICO

VI

Orsini's agents finally found something to get excited about on October 24 1460, when a gathering in *Via dell'Orto* led to concrete plans for a revolutionary intervention in the city two days later, on Friday October 26. The immediate spark was the fact that the younger sister of one of those present, named only as E.M., had been whipped in public for having stolen from her employer, a silk merchant.

This punishment, and the social inequality behind it, could easily have been enough in any case to provoke revolt. But in Florence there was a further level of insult behind the exploitation – a financial level, as we might expect in such a stronghold of international banking. There were, as the English writer Tim Parks usefully explains, two separate currencies in the city – one for the rich and one for the poor. And the value of the gold florins earned by the wealthy was not fixed in relation to the *piccioli* in which the working people's wages were paid. When the merchants who formed the various big city guilds found their profits were down "they encouraged the mint, which was controlled by the government, which in turn was formed mainly of men from these powerful guilds, to reduce the silver content in the *picciolo*. That way it would take fewer florins to pay the same salaries in *piccioli* to the unsuspecting poor".[1]

This was theft from the workers, but it was authorised theft and so did not result in public whippings for those involved. Not in the current bourgeois republic, anyway.

The rebels' plan was for the fakir to start preaching in the *Mercato Vecchio*, where bales of silk changed hands for the gold florins that the workers could never lay their hands on. He would speak about the whipping of E.M.'s sister and the injustice inherent in the Florentine money system and its cynical manipulation by the rich. The others at the meeting, and their associates, would gradually gather to listen to his words as if by chance and without making it clear to the city authorities that a subversive assembly was taking place. When the fakir referred in his sermon to Jesus Christ overturning the money-lenders' tables, this would serve as the signal for the fun to start. Merchants and their wares were to be targeted, as much damage as possible inflicted, and the crowd was then to move rapidly on towards the *Orsanmichele* area, where the red-gowned bankers plied their dubious trade. What happened at that stage would be left to fate, but the rebels presumably hoped that the combination of the fakir's words and their assault on the money-dealing elite would incite a more general revolt amongst the population.

When Orsini received this particular report from his spies he must have felt hugely vindicated and, it seems, rushed off to the city authorities to warn them of the impending revolt. By doing so he succeeded in thwarting the attempted insurrection, but he also missed an opportunity to rid Florence permanently of the man whom he regarded as the source of the problem.

On the day, the signal to revolt in the fakir's speech was also taken as the signal for intervention by the Republic's militia, who stormed out of surrounding streets and attacked the crowd, killing three people including a twelve-year-old girl.[2]

While the authorities did have some proof, from Orsini, that a plot was being hatched, this was not at all apparent to the Florentine public. At the moment of the armed intervention, nothing untoward had yet happened. The fakir had even been referring to the Holy Bible and his condemnation of the dual-currency scam was one that had also often been voiced by the Archbishop of Florence, even if the latter's response was one of charity for the poor rather than anger towards the rich.

While insurrection had been put down on this occasion, the heavy-handed and apparently unjustified intervention by the forces of order merely fanned the flames of revolt still further and, in fact, increased the likelihood that any future attempt at revolution would attract broad support.

Orsini's rush to present evidence of ill-doing to the city authorities had also compromised his spying mission. The dissidents were now aware that they had been infiltrated and would be on their guard. We do not know if the spies themselves were afraid that they would quickly be identified, exposed and challenged, but their reports come to an abrupt halt with the *Mercato Vecchio* incident and there is no evidence as to whether they restarted their infiltration at a later date.

1. Tim Parks, *La fortuna dei Medici. Finanza, teologia e arte nella Firenze del Quattrocento,* 2006.
2. M. Vecino, *Il Rinascimento e l'apocalisse,* 1954.

STRATO CONTEMPORANEO

8

I am sitting in my room, working on the above translation, when suddenly there is a murmur of excitement from the covered terrace of the bar downstairs. There must be football going on, but it didn't sound like a goal had been scored. Some other piece of good news. An opponent sent off? A penalty awarded? Shortly afterwards there is a massive roar. Ah, it was a penalty then! And it's been successfully converted. I can't resist checking on the internet to see who's playing. It's Fiorentina, 1-0 up away to Inter Milan after just five minutes or so at the San Siro. I turn back to my work only to be interrupted again a few minutes later by an even louder roar and the thumping of tables. 2-0. I decide to go for a walk, perhaps with the vague idea of watching the rest of the match, but there are no tables free in the terrace so I walk on across the *piazza*. When I reach the other side, a great shockwave of joy races after me and makes passers-by smile at each other in wonder. 3-0. The *Gigliati* go on to win 4-1 and grab first place in the *Serie A* table, with Nikola Kalinić notching up a hat-trick. I watch the goals on my laptop when I should really be getting on with my translation. But sometimes you have to join in a little bit.

* * *

You can feel the sun in Florence, right from the moment you first step out of doors in the morning, until the moment it disappears behind the rooftops or the surrounding hills. It's not the weak sun we know in England, where even in the summer it takes a while to gather up its daily strength, and is far too easily diluted by the humblest hint of haze or blown away by a mere puff of northerly breeze. By mid-September, sunny days are lovely without exactly being hot. Florence is far enough south that the sun is unconquerable when it rules the sky.

I have in my mind the idea of creating a work of art – contemporary art, of course, since I am a contemporary person. It would consist of four discs mounted symmetrically in front of each other so that they shared the same hub. The first disc, at the back, would be covered with artefacts from the everyday life I have been leading in Florence. *Caffè* receipts, museum tickets, stubs and leaflets. My rather worn street plan of the city centre. The odd paper napkin from a *pasticceria*. Postcards, perhaps. Newspapers. Corks from the bottles of red wine I have drunk. I am picturing it having a five or six-foot diameter. In front of it, leaving enough of a gap so that you could see that the first disc continues underneath, would be the smaller second disc. This would be covered with photocopied pages from *Il fachiro di Firenze*, with pictures of historical scenes from the period, 15th century manuscripts, portraits of some of the historical characters mentioned in Diacono's book. The third disc would be images reflecting the world of the Perantulo stories, engravings of mountains and mysterious ancient cities. The central disc, just a foot across maybe, would simply be gilded. The Florentine sun.

* * *

I have wandered across the *Ponte Vecchio* and am walking alongside the Arno when suddenly I see across the road a sculpture that fills me with excitement. It's not the most beautiful artwork I have seen – the figure it depicts is more of a caricature, a cartoon character even, than anything resembling a human being. But it's the subject matter that interests me – a bare-footed, ridiculously thin bearded man, with long hair and dressed in ragged robes, one arm raised and pointing ahead in the manner of a prophet. Could this be a celebration of *il fachiro* himself? I cross the road convinced that this must be the case, only to make the deflating discovery that it is a representation of *San Giovanni Battista* – St John the Baptist. The *fachiro* really does seem to be someone that Florence would rather wipe out of its history.

* * *

I wake up this morning with nothing in my head other than the translation. I am in such a hurry to get on with it that I don't even linger in the kitchen to eat my breakfast and perhaps have a quick chat with my hosts, as I usually might, but take the coffee, bread and jam back into my room. Neither do I feel the need for a quick walk in the fresh air before I set to work.

After an hour or two, I stand up from the desk and walk out onto the narrow balcony, which stretches between two elegant pillars of this curving neo-classical terrace. The sun is shining outside. The grass in the *piazza* is green, the sky is blue and half a mile away are all the fabulous glories of Firenze. But I am indoors, on my computer, working my way through the translation of this book. I have still been going out, but it's become more of a token effort recently. All the time my head is filled with *Il fachiro*, with the words I haven't quite translated to my own satisfaction and the alternatives that seem to creep into my mind while I sleep.

I have been wondering if it's the mosquitoes that give me guidance. These cunning little beasts – known onomatopoeically in these parts as *zanzare* – bide their time and don't show themselves during the daytime. I suspect they live high, high up in the ceiling and either camouflage themselves against the fresco, pretending to be the mole on a cherub's buttock, or lurk over the top of the window casing where I can't see them, let alone reach them. If I lie still long enough in the evening one will appear, flitting across my field of vision. When it's dark I am dragged out of semi-slumber by a thin buzzing in my ear, as a *zanzara* homes in on its late-night supper, mouth-tube dripping with anti-coagulant saliva in eager anticipation. But before I have time to react, and swipe at them with whatever comes to hand, they vanish again into thin air. I have even looked for them behind the radiators and on the underside of the desk, but to no avail. I did squash one that had stupidly come to rest on the wardrobe door and its little crushed corpse seemed to consist mainly of blood. My blood, I suppose. But maybe, and this is where my theory comes in, maybe they have other people's blood in them too. Maybe it's not just malaria or yellow fever that they can spread around human beings. Maybe there's a positive side as well! This other blood, from sleeping victims a few windows along, will be Italian blood which has passed through the brains and the lungs and the tongues of people who speak Italian properly, authentically. The Italian language is in their blood. Literally. So when the mosquito bites me, it could feasibly – and I'm not going to be writing a scientific paper on this, so don't get too excited – transmit some kind of Italian-speaking and Italian-grasping ability into my bloodstream. This essence travels around my brain while I sleep, and while the carrier continues to gorge him or herself on every uncovered part of my body to be found, this Italian knowledge percolates into my memory of various phrases that I have been translating from the book, unscrambling them into an accurate representation of the original and producing a translation update that pops straight into the inbox of my conscious mind when I next log on in the morning.

I can't think of a better explanation at the moment, put it that way.

I wonder if it's healthy to have allowed myself to sink so deeply into this *fachiro* business. Am I wasting my time here in Florence by devoting my days to translating? I could be out there in the city – or further afield for that matter. Surely this is the time to be embarking on day trips to Siena, Arezzo, Bologna, Ferrara, Pisa... Roma even? Why chain myself to a keyboard at this particular moment, when I have been gifted the opportunity to experience something outside of my everyday existence? Why not wait until I am back home, on a rainy Sunday in a very familiar village where everything is shut? At this rate, I won't even leave Italy with a healthy tan. I wonder if self-deception is involved. I came here with the idea of writing and the hope that Florence would inspire me to do so. But I didn't even give it a chance to work its magic. I launched straight into translating somebody else's book and didn't leave a mental space through which my own thoughts could emerge, or through which I could channel the thoughts of Florence that were waiting here for me to pick up on. I bottled it, it's as simple as that. I was scared that I wouldn't be able to achieve what I so desperately wanted to achieve, but unwilling or unable to face up to that fear of failure. So I masked what was happening by jumping on the first distraction that I came across. It could have been any book with the slightest bit of interest. That was maybe what had been in my unconscious mind while I leafed through the tomes at the stall. What else was I looking for? I came here to write and not to read. If I fancy reading, I have plenty of material with me – books that are a lot more relevant to my general research than this obscure little historical episode. No, I seized upon *Il fachiro* as an excuse, an excuse for not doing what I really wanted to do but which, deep down, I must have feared – or *known* – I was incapable of doing. And, as a result, not only was I achieving nothing in terms of my own writing but I was also wasting this heaven-sent opportunity of *being* in Florence, in absorbing something from the place other than coffee and *zanzara*-saliva.

* * *

I am up and about a little earlier than usual this morning and take advantage of this by heading to the *Santa Croce* ahead of the queues of tourists that have so far put me off stepping inside, although I must have walked past it 20 or 30 times by now.

While it's interesting to take in the memorials to famous Florentines lining the inside of the basilica itself, they wouldn't have been enough in themselves to justify the entrance fee. And while I'm happy enough to pay half-a-minute's homage to Dante or Michelangelo, I'm not sure I want to give the ghost of Niccolò Machiavelli the impression that I'm at all interested in his cynical political prescriptions. But with Giotto's proto-Renaissance decoration of the Bardi Chapel, at the front of the church, my aesthetic taste buds are awoken and the digestive enzymes really get going as I tour around the rest of the premises and soak up the genius of Lorenzo Monaco, Gherardo Starnina, Neri di Bicci, Andrea Orcagna and one of my favourite artists of all time – the incredibly prolific, diverse and long-lived Florentine painter known in Italian as *Pittore Fiorentino*.

When I find myself looking at one or two much later works, enormous over-ripe masterpieces filled with manly torsos and heroically heaving bosoms, I find that my reaction is not the usual one of complete indifference, but one of actual physical repulsion. It comes, therefore, as an especially refreshing and rewarding surprise when I wander off a cloister and discover an exhibition celebrating the 20th century Italian artist Pietro Parigi, who died in 1990 at the age of 98 and whose existence has hitherto passed me by.

His sublimely sparse woodcuts are plainly influenced by the very masterpieces that have impressed me in this basilica that he knew so well, but there is much more to his work than that. He draws his art from the soil as well as from the sacred, from serfs as well as from saints. Parigi's work celebrates the peasants, labourers, beggars and cripples of Italy's towns and countryside. It celebrates seasons, months, festivals, the whole cyclical calendar of life. And it celebrates, by way of its own form, the craftsmanship that had always been united with art, before the one was reduced to practical production and the other to the entertainment of the elite.

Profeta in pregheria (*Prophet in Prayer*) from 1934. *Il potere e la gloria di Graham Greene* (*Graham Greene's The Power and the Glory*), from 1955. *L'alba in campagna* (*Dawn in The Countryside*) from 1924. *San Silvestro ammansisce il drago* (*Saint Sylvester Tames the Dragon*) from 1952.

Here is clarity, radiance, simplicity – all that keeps art close to truth.

I can barely tear myself away from the small museum devoted to Parigi. I realise I am particularly delighted to find that there can be works of art made in the modern era that move me. I feel vindicated by this confirmation that my definite, unwavering preference for the art of the late Middle Ages and early Renaissance – the *Quattrocento* – is not the result of some random nostalgia for an age which I naively imagine might have been better than ours. It is, instead, a physical reaction to the physical reality of the work in front of me, whether it was created in 1436 or 1936. To be enthused by the painting of Orcagna or Giotto is not to be hopelessly out of date, "stuck" in an historical period that has been and gone. It is only to possess an aesthetic, cultural, spiritual taste that happened to be prevalent then but which has not been made any less real and valid by the passing of the centuries. Just because contemporary taste between then and now has celebrated Rubens, Tiepolo, Monet, Warhol or Rozendaal doesn't mean that taste has necessarily improved or that one has some kind of social duty to reflect the artistic *Zeitgeist* by which one is surrounded.

If that all sounds obvious, then try applying the same thinking to philosophy. In this sphere of culture, it is most certainly considered absurd to have a view of the world that would have been shared by people living 700 years ago. We are expected to believe that somehow reality has moved on since then. We are expected to accept that alongside the very obvious *technological* advances made by the human race has come a parallel advance in our *understanding of our own existences*. Personally, it seems obvious to me that the very opposite is likely to be the case – we have focused so much on the material and the mechanical that we have not had the collective time to contemplate deeper matters. But rather than admit this, and try to rectify it, today's intellectual culture smugly insists on denying that there is any such thing as "deeper". People are dismissed as ignorant for not being *au fait* with the latest vapid crossword-puzzle wordplay masquerading as a philosophical insight, "reactionary" for not gasping with admiration at the Emperor's New Post-Visible Clothes.

But what if everything that has happened culturally, metaphysically, philosophically since the Middle Ages – when the early nominalists first made the mistake of confusing reality with the limited, representational, world of language – has been a ghastly mistake, a dead-end in history? Instead of embellishing and surpassing the Great Cultural Fresco of previous millennia, as our vanity insists we have, perhaps we have been busily painting over it, drowning its delicacy and vitality with the clumsy brush strokes of a thick-skinned, greed-glorifying era and in the garish, toxic colours so typical of a society that has thoroughly succeeded in embracing ignorance with arrogance.

Where would that leave those of us who feel, in our dreams and in our blood, that it all went horribly wrong a very long time ago and who stumble with desperate hope towards the light that shines feebly in the long dark tunnel of the *via moderna* through the words and deeds and art of all the poets, revolutionaries and visionaries who have also wrenched themselves free of the chains of their century and spoken the unspeakable?

Where would it leave this world if it became clear that we were right all along, those of us who refused to buy into the scam, refused to abase ourselves to worship all that is clever and kitsch and contemporary, and that it is only the authenticity of our timeless defiance that can pull humankind back from Oblivion's brink?

I feel stronger now, more certain of my certainties, now I know that I can count Pietro Parigi as one of my kind.

* * *

Later I stop off for a coffee on the rooftop terrace of the *Caffetteria delle Oblate* at the library in *via dell'Oriuolo*. It is much used by students and thus reasonably priced, especially since you can enjoy what must be one of the finest views in Florence, looking straight across to the cathedral. The sight of the enormous building is familiar enough to me by now, but I am still taken aback to notice the tiny figures on the viewing platform at the top. The sheer size of the *Duomo* has not struck me as strongly before. Glancing down, I also see that part of the balcony girding the base of the *cupola* is missing, having presumably dropped off at some point. This is the first time I have noticed the defect.

STRATO STORICO

VII

The fakir's involvement in the thwarted attempt at insurrection left Cosimo in a difficult position. Although we do not know what kind of relationship he had established with the stranger, we do know, from the spies' reports, that he occasionally invited him to his home and to Neoplatonic discussions.

Cosimo had a history of supporting wayward, eccentric characters like Brunelleschi and Donatello and may have felt a certain personal pride at being able to accommodate them within his eclectic entourage. Furthermore, any compulsion he might have felt to act against the preacher was mitigated by the circumstances of the incident as it played out and by the fact that the fakir's criticism of the money system reflected the views of the local representative of the Roman Catholic Church. However, some kind of reaction was undoubtedly called for, if only to ease the criticism being levelled at him by Orsini and others for associating with this trouble-maker.[1] Wagging tongues were reminding the

Florentine bourgeoisie that the Medici had famously backed the rebels in the *Tumulto dei Ciompi* – the family still could not be relied upon to maintain law and order, it was implied. It is also possible that Cosimo may have felt personally uneasy about the fakir's political activities – but this must just remain speculation.

In any case, he seems to have taken a leaf out of the Archbishop's book. While the church leader had effectively sent Ficino 120 miles away to Bologna in an effort to lure him away from Platonic heresy, Cosimo effectively sent the fakir 100 miles away to Ferrara in order to cool things down a bit. Of course, he wouldn't have presented it that way and was too canny to even make the suggestion himself. Instead, Cellini reports that the fakir "accepted an invitation from Argyropoulos to spend the winter months at the University of Ferrara and allow the students of that place to benefit from his considerable wisdom".[2]

Of the fakir's stay in Ferrara we have no account – Cellini was not there to note his activities, neither were Orsini's spies, and Sister Sophia was not able to record any of the public sermons he gave there. Perhaps conscious of the risk he had been running with the insurrectionary attempt in Florence, he does not seem to have gone out of his way to make a splash in that city. However, it would seem unlikely that he had not taken the opportunity of getting his message across to the people there, possibly by repeating some of the tales he had told in Florence – he must, after all, have had a limited supply of such fables to impart!

One fascinating, if unprovable, possibility regarding the influence of the fakir's stay in Ferrara comes from an account of the childhood of Girolamo Savonarola, the firebrand rebel priest who was to briefly take control of Florence before being executed there in 1498. This says that "as a boy of eight" he had been deeply influenced by a dream in which he had been at the head of a massive crowd of children who had stormed the churches and palaces of the city, setting fire to them because they harboured "bad and cruel people".[3]

The boy's well-heeled parents feared for his mental health, while his governess apparently declared that a prophet had been born. But his grandfather, a prominent physician, put any such nonsense to rest with the observation that the dream had merely been the result of "exposure to the rantings of a heathen priest passing through Ferrara at the time".[4] Savonarola would have been eight years old in the winter of 1460 and 1461, the very period when *il fachiro* was in residence.

Of course, there may have been more than one heathen priest active in town at that moment, but the intriguing suspicion remains that it was in his exile from Florence, rather than his presence there, that the fakir in fact exerted the most influence on that city's destiny.

1. L. Lezzerini, *La storia degli Orsini*, 1994.
2. M. Vecino, *Il Rinascimento e l'apocalisse*, 1954.
3. F. Roncaglia, *La storia di Girolamo Savonarola*, 1922.
4. Ibid.

STRATO CONTEMPORANEO

9

I am soaking up the splendours of the *Santa Maria Novella* with the sensation of being a cultural sponge that is fast approaching saturation point. There are so many magnificent works of art in this one church, let alone the whole city, that you simply cannot give them all the attention they deserve.

I wonder if this is how these works have contrived to keep their inner energy in a way that is not always the case with Our British Heritage. One or two precious and interesting items, such as might constitute the pulling-power of a typical English cathedral, can be gawped at by so many random people that their power ends up being sucked out of them by the seeing-snapping-owning greed of the day-tripping raiders. But here in Florence there are so many cultural gems that this draining-away of integrity is spread thinly between them, despite the huge numbers of tourists involved. Also, perhaps, the cumulative effect of so much splendid art in one place creates a reinforcing phenomenon, whereby a sort of forcefield is created between all the various items and places which can top up the levels of any particular objects which the visual vampires have singled out for stare-ilisation.

In the *Santa Maria Novella* museum I come across a silver hand, standing upright and cut off from the elbow onwards. All the details are complete, including the shape of the fingernails and the lines on the palm, which sadly I do not have the scientific know-how to read. It is holding a quill. There is a little glass window showing a piece of bone inside, apparently a relic of Saint Rossore, an early Christian martyr. Just across the room is another arm and hand, this time of gilded copper and pierced with an arrow. It contains a tiny fragment of bone supposedly belonging to Saint Sebastian, who also died for his faith at the hands of the pagan Romans. It strikes me as peculiar, almost comic, to see these representations of hands and forearms, on their own without any accompanying body, as if they were the rediscovered icons of some long-lost Hand Religion that once spread across Europe, armed with its gripping gospel of Jesus Wrist and the Glove of God.

The oldest part of the site is *Il Chiostro dei Morti* – the Cloister of the Dead. A noticeboard informs me: "The decoration has only survived in part because a portion of the medieval structure was demolished to make way for the new railway station forecourt in the mid-19th century". I would like to withdraw my previously-stated enthusiasm for Italian railway stations.

* * *

Later I head down to the *Murate* and ask Sofia about a few difficult segments of last night's translating. This has to be done in little bursts of activity, because she's working. I will see her approaching, flitting between the tables with cloth in hand, darting back inside with used cups and plates, and I will keep the sheet of paper with my queries ready to hand, for the moment that she finally alights in my little corner of the yard.

She will enthusiastically talk through the contents of a contentious sentence to my satisfaction – explaining vocabulary, syntax or tone as required – in an extension of the moment which she spends over every table, frozen in the act of wiping up or clearing away. The moment she has answered my query she is on her way again, with an efficient bustle and clatter, and I return to the raw rock face of my translation until the moment that she once again does the rounds outside the cafe and can spend a few minutes with me.

Because our conversation is always so snatched, and because it is very much focused on the book, I know nothing about her other than her name. This obvious and very definite limit to our relationship is beginning to sadden me, as Sofia has become the highlight of my days. On several occasions, when she stands close beside me and leans over to point to the text, I have to physically stop myself from reaching out and touching her arm. Her fingers show no evidence of a wedding ring and I have started daydreaming about asking what she is doing after her shift at the cafe, but somehow the moment never seems appropriate. I know that I am also afraid of frightening her off and losing the invaluable benefit of her help.

After a couple of fairly cloudy days, the sun is shining this morning and I decide to head for the city centre before the rush begins and visit one of the cultural sites I have not yet been inside. The marble of the *Duomo* is shining out at me as I walk into town and I immediately conclude that the day has finally come to brave the crowds and go inside. However, as I enter the *piazza* it becomes apparent that I have badly mistimed my enthusiasm and that this isn't an off-peak moment after all. Great slicks of tourists are drifting around the front of the cathedral and I have to pick my way through them to get any further.

When I reach the door and start to assess the queuing system, I am approached by a smiling individual who suggests, in easy English, that I might like to avoid the "line" by paying for a guided tour in what he has somehow divined is my mother tongue. I politely decline and go round the corner to see just how lengthy the queue is. It goes on and on. It looks like it might loop the whole huge building and come back on itself, like a crowd-sourced Ouroboros, the mythical serpent that swallows its own tail. How would that come about, in terms of a queue? At some point, confusion arises. Maybe some people near the front of the queue get disorientated, distracted by a sudden kerfuffle as an impatient pedestrian scatters the continuity. They haven't being paying attention and think they are still round the back of the cathedral somewhere and have a lot longer to wait, so they shuffle patiently into place behind what they think is the final length of queue before the front door, but what is in fact the back of the very queue which they are heading. Or were heading. Now they are neither at the front nor the back but in the middle of an endless queue of slack-jawed, shorts-wearing, camera-wielding bipedal *bestiame*, condemned by the Kosmic laws of Karma to inch round and round the *Duomo di Firenze* for the whole of eternity without ever getting any closer to grabbing those precious photographs of the world-famous interior.

I try to cut across the crowd and a young Japanese woman suddenly backs towards me as she lines up a shot of the marbled frontage. I step nimbly out of her way only to collide with another amateur photographer coming at me from the other direction. He's a squat, balding man in an oversized white shirt and dark glasses, who looks as if he's covered with a hard day's worth of sweat even though it's barely past breakfast time. Something drops to the ground as we make heavy contact – probably the cover to his camera lens – and he shouts out in anger as if it was somehow my fault that he has ambled blindly and moronically into my path. I don't even deign to turn round and instead I plough on through the masses, now abandoning my usual polite habit of not walking between cameras and the objects of their fascination.

Fuck them, I think. They can all go home with pictures of me in the way. What do I care? What does it matter, anyway, these days, when people take hundreds – no, probably tens of thousands! – of holiday snaps and only end up saving a fraction of them. Maybe I could somehow retrieve all the rejected photos featuring the blurred and darkened outline of an irritated Englishman barging his way rudely in between Todd and Tiffany, between Thibault and

Thérèse, Tobias and Tilda, Takeshi and Takara as each holidaying husband tries to capture one of the Hundred Hippest Heritage Highlights of the Modern World as nobody else has ever captured it – with his own particular wife standing in the way of it, her raw, sunburnt shoulder peeking enticingly from under the flesh-pinching strap of her overloaded shoulder bag.

If I could electronically sweep up all those failed photos, I could run them together and make a little film, a re-animation of my passage across the *piazza* – an indistinct, shadowy, figure flitting like a ghost from a parallel universe. A brief intrusion, a temporary glitch interrupting the real and solid existence of a hard-working, tax-paying, self-loving couple diligently laying down a photographic validation of their contribution to the plane of physical manifestation. Oh! What's *he* doing there? Delete.

As I leave the square and strike out across the city centre with no real idea of where I am going, I decide it would be good to sit down, have a coffee and calm myself a bit. Straight away I see a cafe terrace in front of me and, even though I know it will probably be a bit more expensive than the *Murate* or the *Oblate*, I plonk myself down and order an espresso. As the waiter disappears inside, I notice that there's a menu on the table and pick it up so I can get the change ready to pay him. What? 3.50 Euros? That's three times what I usually pay! For a moment I feel trapped, realising that now I've made my order, it's too late to complain about the price. And then, a split second later, I realise that I don't have to put up with this at all and I simply stand up and walk briskly away from the table, taking care to turn down the first side-street I come to so that I am not within sight of the waiter when he emerges from the interior. I am half-braced for the sound of a shouting voice and running feet, but nothing happens. I am free!

After that, I go straight back "home", make myself a coffee and prepare to get on with another chunk of translation. I am back here a lot sooner than I had imagined and I realise this has become something of a pattern.

Perhaps it's not entirely due to my enthusiasm for the work-in-hand, as I have assumed up to now. Perhaps there's something about Florence itself that is now repelling me, after the magnetic attraction with which it initially led me through its streets, cloisters and museums, pen and notebook in hand.

There is something poisonous about the commercialism of the tourist trade, on top of all the usual boorish business-eering you find in every city, that you cannot simply ignore. Not in the long term, anyway. When I first arrived, the fresh spiritual air that I was breathing in kept the oxygen pumping through my veins and illuminating my thoughts. But the cumulative effect, over several weeks, of all the money changing hands in the city, all the *focus* on the money changing hands, has been building up in my body and reaching dangerous levels. And the stench of financial greed is beginning to creep into my experience of the city, in the same way as the faces of the Florentine bankers began creeping into the paintings of the *Rinascimento* masters. Can a fresco still feel sacred if it is in part a gift to the vanity of the local power-broker? To whom does a painter owe the greater allegiance – his God or his Godfather?

Maybe, I reflect, I am being too negative and my mood has been overly influenced by the 15th century experiences of my "friend" *il fachiro*, as my translation reaches a point where the warmth of his welcome in Florence definitely fades.

STRATO STORICO

VIII

On April 14, 1461, young Sandro Cellini wrote in his diary that *il fachiro* was back in Florence, taking up his old room at the university. He wrote that his friend was "both renewed by his stay in Ferrara and delighted to have returned to this city, where he feels a enormous sense of hope for the possibilities which lie ahead".[1]

This may well have been the mood by which the preacher was gripped when he initially returned, but it was to be short-lived. Seeing the city with fresh eyes seems to have revealed to him again the ugly side which had nearly led to him leaving Florence after just one sermon, but which in the meantime he had managed to overlook.

Cellini records on May 12, less than a month after the fakir's joyful "homecoming" that he was speaking darkly of the state of his adopted city. "He says that there is a great lie at the heart of Florence. He says that the city prides itself on combining all the glories of the past in one perfect present. It boasts the heritage of Rome, the religion of the Vatican, the trading fame of Venice, the philosophy of the Ancients and now, as a result of this great cultural alchemy, the greatest artists in the whole of Christendom. But none of this has any true depth or meaning, he says. *Il fachiro* said to me, and these are his own words: 'The lack-brained Florentine merchants are incapable of understanding any idea other than the *reputazione* of their own family. When they talk of an upward path to purity they imagine that this is something that can be bought with the florins they have plundered'".[2]

It seems the fakir also started to become rather tetchy on a day-to-day basis and had little patience with those who surrounded him. A visitor to Florence in May that year reports coming across "a swarthy and scowling mystic, barging his way rudely through the crowds beside the cathedral, muttering to himself in some strange tongue in which he was no doubt cursing all those with the audacity to be standing in his path".[3]

If the fakir's mood was darkening, it may have been because he was somehow aware that his foes had been sharpening their knives in his absence and that he would no longer be allowed to enjoy the leeway of his first period in the city.

The chief weapon in his enemies' armoury was the rumour mill and by its very nature it is impossible to know exactly by whom it was deployed on any one occasion. However, we might easily assume that Orsini played some part in this. His spies may have stopped providing their daily written reports, but that does not mean that they were not still working for him in some role, perhaps as professional rumour-mongers conducting a whispering campaign behind the fakir's back.

During the Ferrara months, Orsini had had the opportunity to think hard about his strategy in ridding Florence of the preacher. His previous attempt had not only failed but had also potentially increased sympathy for the trouble-makers' cause.

He would not have had to have been a genius to have worked out that painting the fakir as a dangerous revolutionary would certainly turn the bourgeoisie against him, but could prove counter-productive amongst the exploited majority. It would therefore have made sense to have come up with another angle of attack, by which the rebellious influence of the fakir could be countered by provoking hostility against him amongst those who might otherwise have sympathised with him.

It is impossible to state with any authority that Orsini really did hatch a plot to smear *il fachiro* in the eyes of the Florentine public. But the fact remains that three distinct lines of assault began to circulate in the form of rumours, which were duly recorded by a perplexed Cellini and are listed in Vecino's tome.

Firstly, it was said that the fakir had "sold out" to Cosimo and was nothing but his stooge. His sermons against the wealthy were really just disguised attacks on Cosimo's rivals and the whole market incident had been concocted by the Medici to intimidate other merchants and bankers into stepping into line. During his absence he had not been in Ferrara at all, but at one of the Medici villas in the countryside near Florence. There, as a thank-you for helping Cosimo, he had been supplied with a beautiful young mistress and had whiled his days away drinking wine, eating sumptuous meals and making love. The ascetic message of his preaching was a sham, designed to fool the honest working people of Florence.

The second rumour circulating was that the fakir was an Ottoman spy. He had not fled Constantinople at all, but had been sent to Florence by Mehmed II to infiltrate and undermine the most important city in Christendom. He came from the heartlands of the heathen Turkish empire and had played the same role in the capital of the Eastern Roman Empire as he was playing in Florence – confusing and demoralising the population with his blasphemous teachings which were in fact nothing to do with ancient philosophy but were Muslim witchcraft. He was trying to gather around himself an army of followers simply so they could rise up and deliver the city to the Ottoman armies that were threatening to invade Italy. The fakir would open the gates to the Sultan's vicious hordes, who would rape all the woman, kill all the men and take off all the children as slaves to their evil Islamic empire.

The third rumour said that the fakir was

having a clandestine affair with a nun from the Benedictine order of Santa Caterina at *Le Murate*. That was why he had had to leave the city for several months. Again, the related conclusion was that he was nothing but a fake and a hypocrite, whose words might sound powerful and convincing but were ultimately empty.

While Cellini wrote in his notes on May 22 that "surely none will believe these vile slanders", by June 1 he was referring to "the hostility to my friend being expressed by those who have swallowed the lies".[4] The atmosphere was rapidly changing and *il fachiro* would surely have been affected by the negative pressure surrounding him.

1. M. Vecino, *Il Rinascimento e l'apocalisse,* 1954.
2. Ibid.
3. D. Astori, *Testimoni del Rinascimento 1455-1465*, 1976.
4. Vecino.

STRATO CONTEMPORANEO

10

The next day I make an another attempt to get inside the *Duomo*, turning up at lunchtime as suggested by a helpful comment on the internet. It's no better, though the people appear to be arranged in a different way. Instead of one endless queue there are now a series of different queues with no explanation as to where they lead. You presumably have to queue at the *biglietteria* to get a ticket for special parts of the cathedral, like the *cupola* itself. And then you would have to queue again to actually get in. There is another queue at the front, where I looked yesterday, that may be for free entry to the main cathedral, without the need for a ticket. But supposing I waited patiently to get in, only to be told I was at the wrong place and should have got a ticket first? Again, I abandon the whole idea and walk away in disgust.

When I get back to the flat, I leaf through the notes that I've been making as I explore

Florence and realise that two conflicting themes keep emerging. The first is my enthusiasm for the purity and clarity of sacred art and the second is my fascination for the impurity and confusion of the old buildings, walls and rooftops. I pace around the room a little, trying to work out what this means. Do I like the impurity because of its organic, living, quality, as opposed to the potential sterility of the pure ideal? Or was the original artistic and spiritual urge to purity a reaction against a different kind of impurity, a sordid variety that has nothing to do with the mere oldness of crumbling walls and cluttered skylines? If so, the role of the Medici seems to be tied up in all of this, somehow. Were they pure-minded, spiritual individuals who just happened to have become rich through money-changing activities? Or were they money-changers who were desperately trying to buy their own salvation by their patronage of sacred art? The obvious answer, I muse, is that they are not entirely one or the other, but that there is a creative tension between the two aspects of their lives which is also reflected in their home town. Florence's culture was possible because of money, right from the start. Today's tourist trade is surely just that same factor presenting itself in an adapted form? In a way, the whole thing has come full circle. By investing their wealth in art and architecture, Florence's ruling families seemed to be turning away from the material towards the spiritual – or, at least, the aesthetic. But what appeared to be a gesture of cultural philanthropy had turned out to be, from the point of view of Florence as a whole, a shrewd investment that was reaping dividends more than half a millennium later. Money was still pouring into Florence from abroad – from all over the world now – in the form of the endless floods of tourists shuffling across the *Ponte Vecchio* and around the Uffizi.

I lie down on my bed and stare up at the 19th century ceiling-cherub for some help. I am still not happy with the sense I'm making of all this. It's sounding too much like the comfortable clichés they regurgitate endlessly in coffee-table TV documentaries and glossy adverzines. Money and culture cannot be separated, they like to tell us. Ultimately there is no such thing as pure spiritual yearning – it's really little more than a passing fancy, a pretty decoration for the real world of commerce, intrigue and warfare. But I know this isn't true. I can taste the tears famously wept by Fra Angelico when he painted the *San Marco* cells. I can feel the transformative energy streaming out of the gilded gifts of the Magi of the Middle Ages. I can touch the purpose of their existences and it has nothing to do with money, prestige or the family name.

There is something worse going on here than

a mere balancing-out of the one side and the other. One of them is being gobbled up by the other. Art is being consumed by money – even then, back in the 15th century. Looking back from where we are now – lurching helplessly towards the edge of a cliff on board an utterly debased and emptied-out civilization – we tend to notice most in the *Quattrocento* what we are missing in our own age. Purity. Spirit. Clarity. But, in truth, things were already going wrong.

Even the act of transferring spirituality into art perhaps has something suspect about it, I tell myself. Surely that yearning for the infinite is meant to be felt, lived, experienced, rather than reduced, represented, restrained in two-dimensional form? If the aim was to communicate that yearning, it has certainly been achieved, for century after century. But at what cost? If that yearning is embedded in an object – a solid object, an object that can be hoarded and possessed and sold – is it not also betrayed? When you communicate the yearning you are also communicating an acceptance of the context in which it is presented. The authentic and powerful purity that motivated the art has been hijacked, stolen, and its magical force is now harnessed for the impure ends of those who own the object, the gallery, the civilization that can claim the art as its heritage. That is what has been making me so uneasy here. I have been dragged into a world which proclaims that money is not, after all, incompatible with inner beauty. I have been fooled by the cultural recuperation of the Florentine past into half-accepting the enormous lie it dreamt up – that there was nothing unholy, ugly or fundamentally wrong about living for financial profit.

THE WHITE DRAGON AND THE CHESTNUT

Over the long years of his life, Perantulo often found himself drawn to the remote hills of Sevennola, where he would spend the summer months in the great forests of chestnut, oak and pine, wandering along woodland tracks and up to the jagged mountain ridges where he would absorb the Understanding that rose up from the Nature beneath him and descended from the blueness above.

Perantulo loved solitude, but word would gradually spread that he was in that place and by the start of autumn there would be a stream of men, women and youths coming into the forest to seek him out. He did not hide from his visitors. Instead he would reward their interest by coming to a certain place each and every evening where, to the soothing background music of crackling fire and sporadically falling chestnuts, he would tell stories and answer questions.

One evening he told of the White Dragon who lives beyond the Moon and how it became tired of its isolation and yearned to come down to Earth where its enormous strength might be admired by other creatures, where its massive scaly feet would leave great dragon footprints in the soil and where its fiery breath would scorch the leaves in the treetops. It persuaded the Demiurge Diothyn to allow it to leave its heavenly abode for one hundred and one years in order to fulfil its dream of terrestrial being. However, when the White Dragon fell into our world it discovered that here it was the size of a mouse. Its strength impressed nobody, it barely left the slightest imprint on the softest of ground and the fire in its breath was so feeble that it could barely set light to the driest straw. It spent its time avoiding foxes, wild cats, hawks and rats and only dared venture out of its hiding-hole for a few anxious minutes at a time, to seek meagre morsels of food. How it longed to return to the sky-realm where it was a proud and fearless master! But there was no way back. The commitment had been made and there was no longer any way that it could even contact Diothyn, now that it was a tiny earth-bound creature. It knew that it had to see out the duration of its stay on Earth and live out this life for the full hundred and one years. Time passed and the White Dragon carried out its duty, at first with stoical determination but increasingly with some enjoyment as well. It learned to appreciate the world as seen from its lowly vantage-point and to take pleasure in the scent of the earth, the twisting of the roots, the glitter of the dewdrops on the grasses. By the time that 50 years had passed, it had almost forgotten that it had ever been a mighty Dragon from beyond the Moon – the memory had become the faintest shadow of a distant dream. After a further half century, even that awareness had been lost. The only glimmer of connection came when it found itself gazing into the night sky at the dark space in the constellations where it had once lived and wondering what lay up there, so impossibly distant from the hedgerows and ditches that were now its home. Finally the day came when Diothyn made himself known to the Dragon. He explained all that had happened to the bewildered little creature and declared that it would immediately be restored to its rightful position in the firmament.

The Dragon's confusion knew no bounds. It was astonished at the thought of rising beyond the humble life it had experienced for so long and yet deeply afraid of the loss of everything it now possessed. Seeing its discomfort, Diothyn took pity and suggested a temporary compromise. The White Dragon could spend half its time among the stars, as it once did, and the other half on Earth, in the form to which it had become accustomed. When it had experienced both manners of existence for a while, and reflected on their relative merits, it could decide how it wished to spend eternity. The White Dragon readily agreed and divided its time between the two. Every year Diothyn came to it and asked which manner of being it preferred, and every year it replied that it still did not know and negotiated a continuation of its double existence. This all happened seven hundred and seventy thousand years ago and still the White Dragon has not decided between the two realms and straddles both – we see it today beyond the Moon in the night sky and, if we listen carefully, we may hear the scuttling of its scaly feet amidst the pine cones and brambles of its daytime earthly home.

When Perantulo had finished the tale, there were murmurs of approval from most of the dozen people gathered around the fire. The old man noticed that one quiet youth, known as Keppo, joined in the general reaction in such a way that suggested surprise at the outcome of the story, when in fact he had heard it before from Perantulo's lips only ten days before. He smiled to himself at the lad's eagerness to please.

But the dangerous sense of self-satisfaction that had been creeping over the sage was quickly dispelled by the words of a bold-faced girl by the name of Ankya who had arrived at the clearing a mere hour before the story-telling had begun. Perantulo had remarked to himself as soon as she strode self-confidently towards the assembly that she did not wear the face of one who had come merely to listen. As the evening had progressed, and she had said nothing, that feeling had faded a little. Since he had almost forgotten her presence, when she did finally speak, her intervention came as a shock.

"What a load of nonsense you talk, O

Gross-headed Grandfather!" Ankya declared, with undisguised contempt in both voice and eyes. "I came here to discover what you had to say about life and you bombard us with this stupid children's story of a White Dragon from up in the sky and of some invented being called a Demiurge! Do you really expect anybody to take any of that seriously? Are you so afraid of reality that you hide behind this fantasy? If you have a truth to deliver to us, why hide it in this ridiculous wrapping of lies?"

There was a gasp of outrage from the others who had been listening to the tale.

"How dare you?" spluttered young Keppo, rising to his feet in agitation. "How dare you speak to the Sage in that manner?"

But Perantulo held out a hand and motioned to him to be seated. He was frowning, but under his thick brows his dark green eyes were glinting. They were glinting so brightly that all the others turned their faces away from him, shielding their eyes with raised forearms. Only Ankya kept staring at him, her eyes screwed up in defiance.

"Your vanity is to seek truth in your reality and to imagine that reality lies wholly within your truth," he said at last.

"Spare me your riddles, O Age-addled Imposter!" snapped the girl. "Your empty words mean nothing to me".

"Indeed," replied Perantulo with the faintest trace of a smile curling his lips. "Meanings are often best communicated differently..."

He suddenly got to his feet.

"Prepare yourself!" he declared. "I am going to throw a tree at you and I want you to catch it!"

The others present exchanged questioning glances – Perantulo was famed for many extraordinary qualities, but physical strength was not one of them. The girl merely snorted, her features frozen in a dismissive sneer.

Perantulo leant down and, using the sleeve of his woollen robe, carefully picked from the ground a chestnut, freshly fallen and still contained within its bright green prickly casing. In the same movement, he flung it at Ankya, who instinctively reached out to catch it, only to flinch with a cry of pain when the spines pierced her tender young hands.

"Aha!" said Perantulo. "It is real enough, then!"

"Yes, of course it's real," she replied. "But it's a real chestnut and not a real tree,

O Dull-witted Dotard!"

Keppo turned red in the face and looked from Ankya to Perantulo and back with the barely-suppressed desire to intervene and end the insults being levelled at his mentor.

Perantulo merely smiled at the girl. "Why not open it up and look inside?" he said.

Ankya pulled a tired face and trod on the chestnut, squeezing it from its outer covering.

"Well, what a surprise!" she said. "A chestnut!"

"How does the chestnut feel?" asked Perantulo.

She picked up the new-born brown nut and caressed it with her fingers.

"Smooth," she replied.

"And real?" ventured Perantulo.

"Yes, real," Ankya replied. "But still just a nut and not a tree, O Crinkle-skinned Conjuror!"

Perantulo's green eyes glinted. They glinted so brightly that they frightened a nearby pack of foraging wild boar, who scattered in every direction with much snuffling, squealing and trampling.

"Perhaps we have missed something," he said to the girl. "Please break open the chestnut just in case".

Ankya shrugged, stood up and then stamped hard on the nut, fragmenting it into many tiny pieces.

"Look at it carefully!" said Perantulo, as she took the remains into her hand. "And tell me if what is there is real and if you see the tree that I threw at you".

Ankya sifted briefly through the bits of nut and shell and replied: "No, O Senile Story-teller. This stuff is real enough, but there is no tree here!"

Perantulo nodded slowly and waited before speaking. Keppo and the others looked at him with a certain trepidation, as they were not at all sure where all this was leading.

"So," he said in the end. "You have looked carefully at what I have thrown at you. You have discovered it to be real, but have also found that this reality does not contain a tree. And yet had this nut not been broken, and we had planted it in the soil, it could have become a tree. The tree must have been in it somewhere, but just not in the ridiculous wrappings of what you regard as reality.

"Know this, Ankya, that even if I were an invented character presented by a fictional story-teller in an account that was itself a mere fabrication-within-a-fabrication, my words could contain more truth than a lifetime of proven facts listed by someone whose solid physical existence was completely beyond dispute!"

With that, Perantulo's eyes glinted. They glinted so brightly that their light reached up into the night sky, beyond the Moon, and startled the White Dragon itself.

STRATO CONTEMPORANEO

11

Because I am one of the first few visitors to get into the Uffizi museum this morning, at first I have the luxury of a lot of space around me as I soak up the art. I am completely alone, for instance, as I marvel at Simone Martini and Lippo Memmi's astonishing 1330s *Annunciazione,* at Mary reeling in surprise from the physical words of the angel's message that fly towards her and at the delicate depiction of the impregnating breath of the holy spirit, in thinnest, sharpest lines of brightest gold. I have the time to linger in front of Andrea Vanni's *Madonna col bambino* for as long as I like, even to come back for a second look, only just overcoming the urge to sink to my knees in adoration. And there is nobody in my way as I step back to take in the full towering impact of Cimabue's 700-year-old *Maestà di Santa Trinita,* which I reckon must be at least twelve feet tall.

But as I move through the rooms and on to

work mostly from a slightly later period, so the crowds who entered the Uffizi after me begin to catch me up. Great slicks of them block access to works of art as they listen to the drone of their tour leaders. Individuals plugged into audio guides amble into doorways and stay there, apparently blinded as well as deafened to the outside world by the device and incapable of noticing that somebody would like to get past. It strikes me that here is a microcosm of my stay in Florence – a beginning of wonderment and delight at past centuries gradually undermined by the intrusive reality of the crass and contemporary.

Botticelli's *Spring* is a delight to behold in its celebration of the pagan divinity of nature, but his *Birth of Venus*, which attracts more attention, looks sadly faded and empty. I wonder if it's not only the gaze of the pre-packaged holidaymakers that has stolen its soul from it, but also all the worldwide imitation and parody that has used it up and reduced it to the status of an over-familiar cliché. Oswald Spengler writes about exhausted cultures – here we have an exhausted piece of art.

By the time we reach the 16th century the gold has disappeared from the works of art themselves and fled out to the frames in great heavy, ugly, twists of ostentation. The heavenly light, too, has fled from the paintings. Isn't that also what has happened to the feeling of divinity, of connection, that must lie at the origins of religious belief? It was forced out of the interior of the human soul into the overbearing external framework of a pompous religious hierarchy. An intermediary, blocking our experience of the eternal truth. Everything is outside the human soul – ruling it, oppressing it, limiting it. The god within becomes the god above. A god outside of his own creation, outside of his own people, sneering down at their failings. An angry man with a beard ready to punish you for not obeying his orders.

I meet that fierce bearded man in a room devoted to Roman busts. Twice, in fact. Once he is the notoriously aggressive Athenian general Alcibiades, although he apparently he might also be an athlete or a boxer. The other time he is none other than Zeus, the great thundering god of law and order.

I take an instinctive dislike to this man's face. There is raw and brutal arrogance here that I fear, resent and want to blow up with a stick or two of the finest anarchist dynamite.

The thick curly beard seems designed to hide any humanity lurking there, to complete this beast of a man's transformation into a massive and malignant bear who looms up over you and by the sheer potential of His ever-threatened violence insists that you grovel at His great shaggy paws. He is an alpha-bear, an über-bear, an over-bearing bully and tyrant. Our Father Bear, who art in Power.

* * *

I have more time on my hands than usual today, as my hosts have gone away on an overnight trip and so I am not expected back at the flat for the usual early-evening English conversation session. I think that maybe I will take advantage of this by spending even more time at the *Murate*. It is in the back of my mind that if I am still here at the end of Sofia's shift she might linger a little longer with me before she goes home.

When I arrive at the cafe, I immediately know that there is something wrong. Sofia isn't serving on the till, but washing up behind the bar with downturned head. She doesn't appear to notice my arrival and certainly doesn't acknowledge me. I sit outside, despite the fact that the sky is clouding over a little, and get on with my work, while all the time listening out for the clatter that signifies her imminent arrival. But when I hear the signal, and glance round to catch sight of her, I see that it is her colleague – a younger, rather nervous and unsmiling woman – who is clearing the tables. My heart sinks. Sofia has told me that she always makes a point of taking on the outside duties, just to grab a breath of fresh air from time to time, and I've never known her not to do so when I am present.

I carry on with the text, queries unsolved, until the moment comes for the next go-round, but again it is the other member of staff who has emerged into the former prison yard. My impatience gets the better of me and I walk inside with my empty espresso cup and saucer, before the unsmiling woman has had the chance to take it. Sofia is in the same corner, still washing something up. She looks up at me with a terrible expression of sadness and manages a watery half-smile as she says apologetically: "I am sorry. I have been so busy today..." She shrugs, as if to concede that we both know there is more to it than that, but that this is the official story and she's going to stick to it.

"That's OK," I say gently, any fears of a personal snub having been dispelled by the evidence of a deeper, more serious cause. "Maybe later?" I add, and by this I have in mind later on this afternoon, at the end of her shift when for once I will be available, but the look in her eyes as I speak reaches out from the despair within and tells me, somehow, that I can ask for more than this. "Are you doing anything this evening?" I ask, as if acting out a role in a film I have seen many times before. Somehow it seems quite natural when she agrees to come to my lodgings after she's finished work and when I scribble down the address on a little pink slip of paper she digs out from her handbag.

On the way home, I decide that there are three distinct levels to my appointment with Sofia. Firstly, she is coming to help with the translation – that's ostensibly the sole purpose. Secondly, she is obviously experiencing a difficult moment in life and welcomes some sympathetic company. And thirdly... I cannot stop myself from feeling that there is an intangible and powerful connection between Sofia and myself that we are on the threshold of acknowledging.

When it is nearly time for Sofia to arrive, I linger by the window to see if I can spot her approach. I'd like to go and stand out on the balcony, but I don't want to look impatient or over-enthusiastic so I stay out of obvious sight from below. People are streaming across the *piazza*, predominantly in the evening direction, that is to say away from the city centre. Eventually, I spot Sofia. She is clasping the scrap of pink paper and still wearing the simple kind of black dress I have always seen her in at the cafe. For some reason I'm pleased to see that she's not the kind of woman who feels the need to dress up to go out in the evening.

When I let her in the flat, I feel a peculiar kind of pride in her astonishment at the size of the place, as if I were something more than a short-term jobbing guest. I offer her some wine that I've bought but she refuses so firmly that I have the impression she never drinks. She does, however, accept a glass of water and some stuffed olives. We sit down in front of my laptop on the desk, in front of which I have installed two chairs, and work through some of the areas where I am aware my understanding of the Italian text may be a little incomplete.

After a while, noticing that she seems to be in her normal cheerful humour, I decide to refer to the state of mind that has led to her coming here this evening. "Are you all right now?" I ask her. "I noticed that at the cafe this afternoon you seemed a bit upset by something..."

Immediately I see that she has merely succeeded in suppressing whatever it was that has been troubling her. A sudden look of pain fills her face and she immediately puts down the pen with which she has been scribbling notes for the translation.

She smiles, but it's the smile of somebody who isn't really smiling.

"I don't know, Paul," she says. "It's not easy for me. I cannot explain. It's a problem for me, in my life".

"Well yes," I say. "I understand, but you can tell me about it if you want. Maybe that would help?"

She looks at me as if from a great distance,

as if I was talking to her from a place she left long ago, about a world to which she no longer belongs.

"I don't know," she says, pulling away slightly from me in her indecision. Then she rises from her chair and walks over to the twelve-foot-tall windows and gazes out towards the *piazza* for a while.

When she turns round, I see at once that she has decided to tell me something.

"It's about my brother," she says. "Gianfranco is his name, but everyone calls him Bear because he is so big and strong. He's not a good man, although he's all that remains of my family. He was always in trouble when he was a young man, fighting in the streets, arguing with our parents. When he was 20 years old he was in a *banda*, a gang – very violent, fascists. Then later these same people were involved in robberies, in contraband – all sorts of problems. He was already in prison for one year when he was a young man and then two years ago he was found guilty of attacking another man with a knife. 'Stabbing' him, I think you say in English?"

I nod.

"They say he stabbed another man and then this man died. So my brother was a murderer and they sent him to prison for almost 20 years".

"Did he really do it?" I ask, noticing the

doubt implicit in the phrasing of her account.

Sofia laughs in a hollow sort of way, shrugs and holds up the palms of her hands.

"I don't know!" she says. "I think perhaps that he did. He almost told me that he really did this. But for the court, you know, he said that he didn't do anything, it was all a mistake. And now they believe him, maybe! There has been a new investigation and now he will be released while there is more research".

She isn't smiling while she tells me this and I gather it's not entirely good news.

"So this is a problem for you, Sofia?"

"Eh!" she exclaims in that very Italian way. "Now he has nowhere to live and so he is coming to my flat. He will live with me until he can arrange something with his friends or... I don't know".

"I can see that that might not be very convenient for you..."

"Convenient? No, it's not convenient but it's worse than that, Paul," she says, sitting back down and twisting away from me.

When she turns back there are tears in her eyes.

"I don't know what I am going to do," she whispers, almost sobbing. "I cannot stand to have him in my home. He is a shadow over me. For two years that shadow has been gone and I have breathed freely in the sunshine and this makes it worse, you know? When he is in prison I can say that I love him because he is my brother and I can visit him and I can write him letters. But the thought of him in my home, in my room, eating at my table, waiting for me when I finish at the cafe. I do not want him in my life, Paul..."

She lowers her head and lets the tears flow silently down her cheeks. I reach out and take hold of her hand, hanging limply at her side. She grasps mine back and we sit there, in silence, for a time that is more of a space than a length.

Then, suddenly, Sofia pulls her hand free and leaps to her feet.

"I must go!" she declares. "He will be wanting to eat!"

And, with that, she is gone.

STRATO STORICO

IX

We can observe a certain change in the tone of the three remaining sermons that the fakir delivered in this second spell in Florence.

Gone is the simple delight in the miracle of artistic expression of *The Sculptor's Hands*, or the optimism underling *Perantulo and the Water*, with the final "bliss" of union with the sea. Instead, with *The White Dragon and the Chestnut* a defensive note creeps in to the fakir's storytelling, which develops into the melancholia of *The Sadness of the Singer* and finally the nihilistic rage of *The Whirling Dance*. Can we perceive an influence from real life in the way that the fakir has his alter ego Perantulo accused of peddling "lies" and being an "imposter" in the *White Dragon* tale? Was the critical young woman Ankya with her "dismissive sneer" based on someone *il fachiro* had encountered in real life, just as the appreciative young student Keppo was perhaps modelled on Cellini?

The rumours against the preacher were therefore effective not just in turning a portion of public opinion against him, but in affecting his state of mind and destabilising him to the point where he was capable of delivering his ill-judged final sermon.

A third success of the various slanders against him, whether or not they formed part of a concerted campaign, was to alienate the two figures whose influence had been the most decisive to the fakir's status in Florence – John Argyropoulos and Cosimo Medici. It appears, from a letter written by Argyropoulos and cited by Badelj, that the pair spoke of the preacher one afternoon in late May, while the Greek was discussing the education of Cosimo's grandson Lorenzo, later known as *Lorenzo il Magnifico*, to whom he had been appointed tutor. He stated: "Cosimo agrees with me that the eccentric in our midst is becoming altogether a liability".[1] Particularly interesting, however, are two sentences which appear later in the letter which suggest the significant involvement of a third person's viewpoint in their deliberations. The first of these states: "As Marsilio has pointed out, the great Platonic Academy which we are founding here in Florence cannot afford to be tainted at birth by association with folly of this kind". The second says: "The rumours of dissipation and treason, as passed on to me by Marsilio, cannot lightly be overlooked".[2] In other words it was Marsilio Ficino who passed on the malicious rumours about the fakir to his tutor and it was Marsilio Ficino who suggested that the preacher's influence could undermine the reputation of the Platonic Academy, a project which he knew to be so dear to Cosimo.

We have already noted that Ficino was wary of the fakir on account of his divergent metaphysical and social viewpoint, as well, perhaps, as out of a sense of personal resentment. While it would be unreasonable to suggest that a philosopher of his ability and standing would stoop to inventing false rumours about a rival, it is certainly conceivable that he would have taken some satisfaction in gathering and repeating them in order to advance his own cause.

The result of the conversation between Cosimo and Argyropoulos was that the fakir was no longer invited to Cosimo's home or to his Platonic gatherings and, more seriously on a practical level, he was given notice to quit his university room.

On hearing the latter news, Cellini naturally invited the fakir to return to his family home across the Arno and assured him that there would be no shortage of offers of lodging amongst his friends and neighbours. *Il fachiro* was, however, reluctant to take up the offer and instead spoke of "leaving Florence for once and for all"[3] – a plan that we now know he would have done well to have seen through. As the deadline for his departure from the university drew closer, he showed no signs of making the move of his own accord – a development which worried Cellini, who had no wish to see his mentor humiliated by the process of physical

215

eviction.

The preacher had not abandoned his vocation in the meantime and was still capable of attracting large and enthusiastic crowds, despite the mud being flung at him by the city's gossips. Indeed, a letter from Orsini to his cousin on June 11 paints a picture of a city on the brink of revolution: "Great mobs gather in the streets to hear the words of the foreigner and others of his kind. The crude roaring of their uncouth voices forces me at times to have the servants shut all the windows in spite of the heat. After they have been fired up by all the rabble-rousing talk, they roam the streets in ugly bands – women as well, and children of ten or twelve years of age, chanting and screaming and singing vile songs of contempt for those who have created the wealth and well-being that they would squander in their idle drunkenness and debauchery. 'Long live the *popolo* and death to rich tyrants!' they yell in their ignorance. Anyone that they pass in the street who is not as low as they are, who is dressed at all smartly and whose skin is not grimy with neglect, is subjected to abuse and even physical assault. A friend of mine, a countess, was followed home from the theatre last week and pelted with rocks as she entered the building. The ruffians broke three windows and smashed into smithereens an elegant and expensive statue at the entrance to her driveway. How long must we endure this anarchy? What is being done to combat this menace by the so-called protectors of the Republic? How can we tolerate in our midst a foreign agitator sent to whip up anger and dissolve the traditional social bonds that hold this city together? Something must be done, dear Cousin! Somebody must act!"[4]

The increasing hostility experienced by the fakir did not therefore mean that he had lost the support of those who had previously rallied to his rebellious speeches, but simply that his opponents had succeeded in mobilising a hitherto dormant section of the population against him. The rumours of Muslim conspiracies and personal hypocrisy were designed to appeal to the fearful and reactionary element in public opinion that is often activated by those in power when they are in direst need. There was an increasingly tense polarisation of Florentine society, of which the fakir found himself very much the focus.

1. M. Badelj, *Giovanni Argiropulo e le origini dell'umanesimo*, 1948.
2. Ibid.
3. M. Vecino, *Il Rinascimento e l'apocalisse*, 1954.
4. F. Lezzerini, *La storia degli Orsini*, 1994.

I have been thinking again about the *Quattrocento* and wondering how all the beauty that it painted could have been so quickly tainted by its exposure to money. It strikes me that there was nothing necessary or inevitable about this process. The sacredness that has been shining into my soul from the great works of art I have seen here is no less authentic because of the way it was corrupted and recuperated. It was a genuine attempt at cultural and spiritual renewal. Its failure was nothing to do with its own content or essence, but was down to the greater strength of those forces pulling humankind in the opposite direction. The delicate little wave of rebirth rippling across the European waters was simply overwhelmed by the great tsunami of greed-worship that was to shape the centuries to come in every imaginable way.

The same thing has happened time and time

again, it seems to me. On each occasion we ascribe the failure of a renewing-movement to its own ideals or personalities and we simply don't see that it was never allowed to reach up from the soil of its conception, to branch out and blossom, because when it was still a tiny green shoot it was crushed to death by the juggernaut transporting us all into the modern era.

Because this crushing is complicated, and involves a destruction of the renewing-movement from within as well as from without, we are blinded to what has happened and we forget the glorious potential that existed at the beginning of the English, French or Russian revolutions, in the outbreak of protestant rebellion against Rome, in romantic anti-industrialism, in the early days of socialism, in the passion of the original anarchists.

These attempts at changing the world for the better did not fail – they were defeated by the dominant direction in which society has been dragged for so long. They were submerged and subsumed by the slick of coal, plastic and depleted uranium that has been blown up on to every last beach on the planet by the stinking breath of the Dark Prince of Progress.

What we shouldn't forget, though, is that these little waves of potential renewal will continue to be created by our society as long as humankind exists. The desire is part of our nature, our essence, and is born again in each new generation, regardless of how brutally previous rebellions were put down by authority, regardless of how effectively the system has hitherto neutralised dissent with perpetual brain-paralysing propaganda.

The revolt will keep coming, again and again, until eventually one of these waves of renewal will be so strong, or the dominant counter-flow so weak, that it can't be stopped and it prevails. Renewal will no longer be an idea, but a reality.

And when people in the future look back at those who rebelled in the past, they won't see them in the same way at all. They won't see ridiculous failures, sad misfits, idle day-dreamers pointlessly trying to hold back the Course of History. They will see them as the heralds, the precursors, the prophets of what was to come, men and women who were ahead of their times, not behind them. They will see clearly that to fight a pernicious plague that risks destroying humanity is not simply to look back fondly to the days before the plague arrived but also to look forward eagerly to the day when it has gone. They will see all the rebels and romantics and revolutionaries of our era for what they truly are – visionaries, guiding stars, angels come to lead us to a brighter future. They are the sweet damp scent of grass and trees and rivers that wafts through the open window and eases the restless sleep of she whose dreams are choked with concrete. They are the sharp and energising trill of birdsong in the darkness of the dying night. They are the first shimmering sight of the crown of the sun's head as it rises to its birth between the horizontal labia of earth and sky. They are our hope and our perennial inspiration.

* * *

I have the same nightmare for the third time — the sense of menace outside the door of the flat, the lurking figure in the hallway. Only this time it goes a step further and I see who it is out there, who has been out there all along. It is not a human being at all, but a bear. A huge heavy-limbed bear with the hard eyes of a killer and a knife poised to strike at my heart. I awake in a state of fear and find myself in the midst of a great shuddering. It is as if war has broken out and the room is resonating to the deep and mighty throbbing of dozens of 200-ton tanks rumbling past in the street below, or as if I am on board an enormous ocean-going ship whose mighty engines have been thrust violently into reverse as it manoeuvres into port. Or, maybe, it strikes me, as if a murderous bear the size of a mountain was shaking with rage in the city outside. The massive windows are rattling frantically in their frames. I am aware that I myself and everything inside me form part of this powerful oscillation. The world does not seem as solid as usual. Then suddenly, it stops. Everything is still once more. It was a minor earthquake – nothing to get excited about in these parts. I look for the time and find it is just after 3am, then go back to sleep.

THE SADNESS OF THE SINGER

Once Perantulo's tireless feet took him hundreds of leagues away from his homelands towards the distant northern coast, from where he sailed across to the rain-lashed and verdant archipelago of Prydina. There he spoke with the wise women of that place, whose fame had reached him many years before. They were said to be the inheritors of an ancient Knowledge stretching back to the days of the great stone circles that littered the rounded hills of this cold land so remote from the great civilizations of the Central World.

After he had spent a year and a day with the Sisters of the Tree Temple, he and they had both learned more than most of us have the privilege of learning in a lifetime.

Perantulo set off again towards the port of Gwalaish, from where he would find a boat to ferry him to the mainland, and he decided to take the trail that led there along the coast.

The sun shone fresh in his face and the wind dazzled his eyes as he stopped on the clifftop to watch the waves racing towards the shore and crashing into whiteness on the rocks below.

And then, gradually, he became aware that beneath the thundering of the sea and the shrieking of the gulls there was another sound enticing his ears.

It was the sound of a woman's voice, singing. And the singing was both painfully beautiful and marvellously sad.

Perantulo peered over the cliff to try to ascertain where it was coming from. Seeing nothing, he found a small path winding its way downwards and, despite slipping twice on the crumbling surface, he managed to descend to the beach from which the melody seemed to be emanating.

Guided by the voice, now clearer and more bewitching than ever, Perantulo clambered over some rocks on the edge of the shore, paying no heed to the fact that his robes were wettened in the pools of seawater, and found his way out to the very end of a craggy promontory, where there sat the singer herself.

She was beautiful to behold, of that there was no doubt. Her hair was long, her body slender, her features sculpted with finesse. And if her face was lined with age and wearied with experience, that somehow only deepened its captivating allure.

But her appearance was of little import compared with the astonishing magnificence of her voice. Her song flowed and ebbed and surged like the ocean itself and she caressed each phrase with the purity and tenderness of a moonbeam lighting the crisp white crest of a black nocturnal wave.

The words spoke of a deep and mournful sadness, although in truth they were not needed except as the vehicle by which the music could express itself – the story they described had already been told by the melody and by the way it was breathed forth into the world.

As he listened to the woman, Perantulo could not stop himself from beginning to gently weep. He wept so sincerely that the gulls circling above all started weeping with him and a little shower of salty bird tears drifted down on him and on the singer.

This caused her to look up and around and when she saw Perantulo standing there she was ashamed and stopped her performance, which had been intended for nobody but herself and the horizon.

"O Nightingale of the Rocks," said Perantulo to her. "Please do not stop your singing on my account. Never before have I heard such a sublime and moving rendition!"

"Thank you, O Wanderer," said the woman, blushing at the compliment. She asked him what he was doing in those parts and, when he had told her, she introduced herself as Engma. She explained that she lived nearby, in a cottage on a little cove where she grew vegetables and made bread to sell at the market.

Engma launched into an account of various details of her daily life and some amusing incidents related to them.

Perantulo listened patiently to what she was telling him, but it was not what he was interested in hearing. Finally, he said to her: "Engma, your singing was the best that I have ever heard and stirred my heart even more than the Wailing Women of Khovvo or the Choir of the Invisible Sun that performs publicly only once in every seven years at the Black Hand Festival of Mesqa-Murro. But it left me wondering about the nature of the immense sadness from which it has arisen. Could you bring yourself to tell me about it? Come, sit next to me here on the rocks".

The woman hesitated a moment. Could she talk openly to this old stranger? And then she saw in his eyes that of all the strangers in the world, this was the one that she could trust. And so she sat down beside him and started to talk.

Engma's story was not a happy one. It was an account of a lonely childhood starved of affection, of a great love affair that went horribly wrong, of two children that she bore and nurtured but were swept away by the pitiless seas of Fate. And now she was alone, the years were passing fast and she was ever more aware that the tide of mortality was creeping up and ready to lap around her feet.

Such was the pathos in her words that Perantulo found himself moved more than he had ever been moved by such a description. Silently, he began to weep. And he wept with such simplicity that the cliffs above him began to weep too, and salty water poured out of their every crevice, forming a torrent that rushed its way down the beach and into the sea.

As he wept, and she spoke, he reached out his hand and took hold of hers. They gripped tight on to each other and each felt they would never let go.

Finally she asked him: "Is there no cure for my sorrow, O Listening Wanderer from Afar?"

"O Songbird of the Shore," said Perantulo, "your sorrow is real and cannot be explained away by any words, but the ancient teachings can help us to understand and accept its source. I have been talking of these very matters here in Prydina with the Sisters of the Tree Temple and we found that the wisdom of the ancestors tells the same tale here as it does in my own homelands".

Engma looked at him silently and still held fast to his hand.

"First of all," he said. "Although you complain that you are alone in the world, you forget that this is true of each and every one of us! The daily proximity of any number of other people cannot remedy this state of affairs. Indeed, she who is most surrounded by others in the external world often feels more alone than ever on the inside".

Engma nodded without saying

anything. She had understood.

"Secondly," continued the mage, "you are very aware of the passing of time, but this awareness is based on an illusion!"

Now, however, the singer could not help speaking out. "How so?" she asked, pulling her hand away from Perantulo's.

"It is the same kind of illusion that makes people talk of the sun rising and setting," he said, gently taking her hand back in his. "Why do we use this form of language, when we know full well that it's not the sun that moves, and crosses the sky, but the Earth on which we stand that rotates in and out of the sunlight? Likewise, why do we talk of time passing when it is in fact we who pass through time? And why do we regard ourselves as passive victims of some great crushing external force when our passing is our living, our passing is our acting in the world, our contribution to the forming of the world? If we did not stride through time, we would achieve nothing. We would be frozen images of humanity, mere effigies deprived of the dimension that gives us existence".

Engma smiled at his words.

"Thirdly," concluded Perantulo. "You have told me that you fear death. And yet, at the same time, you dislike being alone.

This makes no sense! When we die, we are reabsorbed into the rest of the universe. Our individuality exists no more, but our essence becomes at one with everyone and everything else around us. You could hardly be less alone than this!"

A little laugh came from Engma's mouth – or perhaps from her nose because she barely parted her lips.

They both sat there for a while as the waves crashed, the tide crept up the beach and the horizon raised itself closer to the sun.

Finally Perantulo asked her: "Will you not sing to me again, Engma, before it becomes too cold, too dark and too wet to remain here any longer?"

At that, Engma stood up and stepped on to the rock where she had stood before and she began.

Again it was a song of desolating radiance that was blown by the breezes into the gathering gloom of the ocean. And this time it was touched by an even darker and richer grace than before, an exquisite aching that surged and soared and seared into the soul.

Perantulo wept. His weeping was so heartfelt that the whole of the Archipelago of Prydina wept with him. The people wept, the animals wept, the trees wept, the hedges and the grasses wept. The walls of the Temple wept, the ancient standing stones wept, and the rolling hills wept too. All these tears welled up, flowed from the isles in every direction and poured into the ocean, giving it the salty quality that it retains to this day.

When Engma had finished her song, Perantulo addressed her.

"O Skylark of the Seas!" he said. "You have truly surpassed yourself. Tell of me of the sadness that now informs your melody!"

"O Prophet of the Ever-Present," she replied. "My song is no longer informed by the loneliness of my individual life, but by the loneliness of every spark of light which has scattered apart from the great furnace of unity. My song no longer bewails the passing of time, but the weakness of humanity in not embracing more courageously the existence that is granted us. And my song no longer fears death, but laments that each personal existence so embittered by separation must inevitably come to an end a split second before it can taste the joy of reunion".

Perantulo left the island the next morning and never returned, but Prydinian music remains known for the rare and

spiritual subtlety of its mellifluous melancholia.

STRATO STORICO

X

We do not know what was in the preacher's mind
when he decided to give his final provocative
sermon on the evening of Tuesday June 18, 1461.
The choice of the date is presumably linked to the
fact that he was to be expelled from the
university room the next day. Was he intending
the speech to be a farewell to Florence, after
which he would gather his little bundle of
belongings and head back off into anonymity in
the wider world? Is this why he chose the
symmetry of delivering the sermon in the *Piazza
del Duomo,* scene of his first appearance in the
city some 19 months previously? It would
otherwise seem a strange choice. If he was
hoping to spark a popular uprising with his
words, would it not have been easier to have done
so in the more receptive territories across the
Arno? On the other hand, any such revolt would
have been in exactly the right place to attack the
great symbols of Florentine power, so maybe that
was all part of the plan. And, of course, his many
supporters were aware in advance that he would

be preaching outside the cathedral that evening. This advance information evidently reached as far as the convent at *Le Murate* and Sister Sophia turned up to record one of his sermons for the seventh and last time.

It is not hard to understand the motivation behind the sermon's fairly direct attack on Cosimo and his circle. The fakir can never have felt completely comfortable in such circles. The rumours suggesting he was Cosimo's obedient lapdog would have intensely irritated him and he may have felt that they needed countering in the strongest possible way. Now that Cosimo had withdrawn his role as an informal protector, there was nothing in the way of a statement putting some distance between the two of them.

However, we cannot fail to come to the conclusion that the decision to deliver that particular sermon at that particular time and in that particular place was an enormous mistake. It was a mistake because the fakir essentially wiped himself out of Florentine history in one fell swoop. There was no popular uprising for which he would be remembered and he was not one of those martyrs whose execution at the hands of the authorities is etched into the public mind for generations to come. He just disappeared from the Florentine scene in the midst of much confusion and uncertainty as to what exactly had happened.

This made it easy for his various enemies to achieve what they had wanted all along – for him to be forgotten. Orsini didn't want the people to remember the inspiring metaphysical justification that he had provided for their insurrectionary desires. Cosimo didn't want the leading lights of the city to recall his own role in welcoming someone who was so clearly hostile to their activities. Ficino, in particular, would have been relieved that he now had a clear field to develop Neoplatonic philosophy in the direction he saw fit, without competition from what he would have regarded as the primitive paganism of the preacher. He not only went on to establish a permanent Platonic Academy at the *Villa di Careggi*, but also achieved priesthood and a good degree of respectability, despite his brief brush with accusations of heresy.

We might also say that Florence got what it wanted and so did the new European capitalist society to which it in many respects gave birth. It is difficult to imagine what would have happened if it had been the fakir's rebellious version of mysticism that had caught hold of European imagination in the fifteenth century. It is difficult to picture the direction our civilization might have taken if the *catena aurea,* the golden chain of ancient hermetic thought passed on by Gemistus, had not been entangled with Roman Christianity by the cunning theological craft of Ficino, his friend Giovanni Pico della Mirandola and their successors. It is difficult to imagine what would have happened if the liberating and empowering concept of a living and all-inclusive universe had fed into the main flow of popular European thinking and reunited with the old ways of seeing the world that had been forced underground by the Christian Church, if it had fuelled a powerful holistic philosophy of complete and uncompromising rejection of all so-called authority, whether divine, royal or plutocratic. There continued to be sporadic outbreaks of revolt along these lines, but the philosophy behind it always seemed corrupted in some way and too easily turned into new forms of intolerance and reaction – take the narrow and unpleasant puritanism of Savonarola's brief 1490s regime, for instance, or the reactionary authoritarianism of the "rebel" Martin Luther in the 1520s.

We might conclude that a radically different way of seeing the world was unable to take root because the development of modern society dictated that this could not be so. The mercantilism of the Renaissance needed a philosophy that supported its activities and not one which challenged its material shallowness. Capitalist society and the associated growth of state control needed ways of thinking that encouraged obedience and conformity. The Roman Empire had already demonstrated how Christianity could easily be adapted for this purpose and now Ficino *et al* showed how ancient metaphysics could also be recuperated and co-opted for the same cause. The wisdom of *Pansophia* was no longer a threat to wealth and power if its knowledge ceased to be universal and became instead an "occult" fetish jealously guarded by a social elite for the purpose of their own entertainment and self-advancement.

The only way that the philosophy expounded by the fakir could have triumphed was if it had succeeded in destroying the nascent bourgeois civilization that could never allow it to flourish in all its free and egalitarian glory, if the vision in his last story had come true. Perhaps he knew this, deep down. Perhaps that is what led him to the square outside the Cathedral on that muggy summer night in 1461. Perhaps this was his great gamble, a last throw of the dice to determine the direction which would from now on be taken by Florence, by *il Rinascimento*, by the new Europe. In that case, his total failure should not blind us to the nobility of his intent.

The clouds were already building up when *il fachiro* began his address and a rumble of thunder was echoing in the Tuscan hills. Before he had picked up the pace, a patter of sparse but heavy raindrops was falling in the square. People began to retreat into doorways to avoid getting wet. Already, the chances of the fakir being able to provoke a popular uprising were severely diminished. People don't take so readily to the streets when it's raining. With hindsight, we can suggest that he should have cut his losses at this point, as some of his listeners backed away almost out of earshot and attention switched slightly from his oration to the coming storm. He could have changed tack, told a different story, kept his powder dry and held back his rhetorical fireworks for another occasion when they were more likely to spark off the city's revolutionary potential.

But he didn't. He carried on regardless, even as the rain suddenly became much heavier and lightning flashed in the dark billowing skies above the *Duomo*. Nearly everyone scuttled for cover. Cellini did not do so, of course, and neither did Sister Sophia. For the first time Cellini notes her presence, having perhaps even only been alerted to her existence by the unfounded rumours that had been circulating: "A nun stood in the teeming rain, huddled over quill and paper, diligently trying to record the words of our friend, although how she can have reproduced them with any accuracy in such circumstances is beyond me".[1]

As the downpour became torrential, there remained in the open *piazza* only those who really wanted to be there, including a few diehard supporters of the fakir and a group of men who started heckling him, taking up the various allegations circulating against him, according to Cellini. Whether these men stayed out there in the rain to insult the fakir because they felt so strongly about the issue, or whether it was because they were being paid to do so, we cannot tell.

As the fakir's fiery last sermon reached its climax, so the gaps between the lightning and the crashes of thunder became shorter. A sudden wind whipped up and drove the rain into the doorways, clearing even more of the preacher's audience away from the square. Still the foreigner persisted, shouting at the top of his voice now, to make himself heard above the elements. And then, as he finished his tumultuous sermon with the words "infinite and eternal fire", there occurred what Cellini described as "a kind of miracle, though from where it was sent it is hard to define, as its consequences were more in the nature of a disaster".[2] A bolt of lightning hit the great dome of the cathedral with a great crack that could be heard 20 miles away and, at the very same moment, the ground shook with one of the earth tremors that regularly affect the Italian peninsular. We can imagine that the resulting effect must have been little less than apocalyptic. In the confusion, a scuffle broke out between the few remaining supporters and opponents of *il fachiro* and from the melee two men, hostile to the preacher, broke away and rushed across the *piazza* towards him. Seeing their approach, he turned tail and disappeared round the corner and out of sight of the watching Cellini. The student set off after him, but couldn't initially find his friend or his pursuers. A search of the dark, deserted and rain-lashed streets soon led him to discover, however, the fakir's dead body slumped in an alleyway "the blood trickling from his chest being washed into the gutters by the streams of water flowing around him as he lay".

The preacher had been stabbed. At first, it was assumed that the men who had run after him must have been responsible, but later it emerged that a woman whose home overlooked the scene of the murder had been alerted by the sound of shouting and, on running to her upstairs window, had seen the preacher being confronted by "a mountain of a man".[3] She had witnessed him plunging a dagger into his victim's chest and then making off, but she had not caught sight of his face. Popular wisdom had it that the fakir had been ambushed by a man known locally as Orso, rumoured to be the long-lost husband of Sister Sophia of *Le Murate* – potentially with the co-operation of the pair who had chased him from the cathedral square. Another version unearthed by Lezzerini, however, states that the nun was in fact the sister of the aristocrat Orsini and had devoted her life to Christ after her two children had died of a mysterious illness and their father had disappeared. By this account, the heavyweight who killed the fakir was in Orsini's pay, his motivation being based on family dishonour rather than any political motive.

Five and half centuries later, there is no chance of us being able to discover the truth about a crime which remained unsolved at the time. All that matters to us is that the Fakir of Florence, the subject of this account, was dead and that therefore this story has come to its end.

1. M. Vecino, *Il Rinascimento e l'apocalisse,* 1954.
2. Ibid.
3. Ibid.

13

I save the file on my laptop, back it up on to my memory stick and lean back in my chair. That's it, as far as the main text goes. Just the final Perantulo story to translate and then I will have finished the whole book – and I still have three days in which to do so. I allow my mind to start wandering ahead to whom I might ask to read through the text, whom I might approach to write a foreword, what the best publishing options might be. I even consider how I will phrase the dedication to Sofia at the start of the book, emphasising the contribution she made to my understanding of the Italian original.

Suddenly, a thought strikes me. I will need permission to publish the translation! I can't believe I haven't already considered this. It must be because I've never been in this position before, of wanting to publish something that's not actually my own work. I tell myself not to panic as I check in the book for the name of the

publishers. Ah yes, that's it. *Pansophia, Firenze.*
All I have to do is get in touch and ask them –
they'll probably be delighted that someone is
showing an interest. They may even be
interested in publishing my English translation
themselves!

I look for their address on the internet but
find nothing. Not in Florence, anyway, though
there does seem to be a PanSophia Press in the
Netherlands. I've already searched for the
author's name and discovered that he was a
scholar born in the 8th century, so presumably
it's just a pseudonym. This is awkward, but I'm
sure there will be a way of finding the
publishers, especially since I am here in
Florence. At least I've realised my omission at a
point where I can still do something about it.

I stand up, walk to the window and look
across to the road leading into the city centre. Of
course! The bookseller! He seemed to know
something about the book. He should be able to
point me in the right direction. It's only three
o'clock, so I've got plenty of time before the five
o'clock English-language session.

I gather my things together – including the
book itself, to prompt his memory – and make
my way out of the flat and towards the centre of
Florence.

When I get there, the bookseller is deep in
conversation with another man, a heavily-

moustachioed octogenarian incongruously wearing a thin nylon branded training top. I pretend to be taking an interest in the books on the stall while I am waiting, but I am not in the mood to even take in their titles. I am impatient to put my mind at rest by getting in touch with the publishers.

As I circle impatiently around, waiting for this interminable conversation to end – it seems to involve technical details of the Italian airforce during the Second World War – I feel a single drop of water fall on the crown of my head.

Finally, they have finished and I move swiftly towards the stallholder, book in outstretched hand.

"Ah! You want to buy, yes?" he asks.

"Err, no, I already..." I begin, then see that he is laughing.

"Yes, yes, I remember, I remember! I am only joking! How can I help you, Sir? It's a very interesting book, yes? Very much imagination!"

"Interesting, yes," I reply. "But I don't know about imagination – it did all really happen, after all, no matter how amazing it seems!"

He looks at me strangely and raises his hands, as if in self-defence.

"No, no..." he says. "It's not a true story. It's a *romanzo*, a fiction. I think I tell you – it's *una bella storia!*".

I feel as if the ground has turned into water

under my feet.

"B-b-but... I don't understand! There are real people in there. I've checked some of it on the internet. And there are sources mentioned, academic papers... Look!"

I am now desperately flicking through the book to point this out, as if he might suddenly realise the error of his ways and save me from this devastating truth.

"Yes," he says, barely glancing at it. "Yes, he is a very cunning man. Some of these books I know are real – I have some here if you are interested! But others are fantasies. He invented them, borrowed the names of footballers from Fiorentina – you can find them if you look! And then he mixed all together to create a confusion!"

I am speechless. I just don't know what to say. I feel so stupid.

"Thanks," I say. "Thanks for telling me. He certainly is cunning. It was very convincing!"

He waves cheerily as I head back off up the road, but the fake smile fades from my face the moment I turn away from him.

It's starting to drizzle with rain now, but I don't even care. I am solely and absolutely involved in my shame and anger at being the gullible victim of an obvious literary hoax. And of course it's not just a question of my bruised pride at having admitted to the bookseller that I thought it was real. I could move on from that, smile at my foolishness and push the whole incident to the back of my mind. No, I've actually spent a month of my life lovingly translating an historical lie!

"The Fakir of Florence," I spit to myself. "More like the Faker of Florence. The Fucker of Firenze. The Fucking Faker of Fucking Firenze. The Fucking Faking Fuck-Faced Fucker of Fucking Fake Firenze!"

A mild-looking hand-holding couple of middle-aged Italians coming in the opposite direction are staring with open mouths at my no-doubt distorted, scowling, muttering face, but I don't care. I keep walking in a straight line towards them, forcing them to break apart and let me through between them.

I am burning with indignation at the effort I have wasted on this affair. I could have been getting on with my own work – the various projects I had lined up. I could have been writing something completely different. I could even have been gently enjoying myself wandering around Florence, even taking day trips to nearby towns and cities. And I sensed that all along, somehow! I already had this conversation with myself, when I still thought the book was real. Even then, I *knew* that it was a waste of time, but I didn't listen to myself. What I have I achieved, after a whole month here? Nothing!

As I stride on through the drizzle, though, a

little voice begins to make itself heard through the self-hating rage which is noisily filling my head. "Was it *really* a waste of time?" it is asking. "Is this *really* a complete disaster? Isn't there something here, something you haven't yet put your finger on, that you have forgotten in all this?"

Just as I reach the street doorway to the flat and am placing the key in the lock, I realise what it is that I have overlooked. The story was not real, but it is still a good story! I enjoyed it, I was entertained by it as well as fooled by it! It's a novel, an intriguing novel, and I have just translated the whole of it! Ultimately, what has changed? I can still approach the publishers and ask for their permission to bring out my English translation of their novel!

I pause in the doorway, key in lock, and allow myself a smile. Idiot! Over-reacting as usual. I just have to pop back to the book-seller and ask him what I meant to ask him in the first place. And then take it from there. First, though, I'll fetch my plastic raincoat from upstairs.

The rain is getting a little heavier as I reach the book stall *piazza* and the seller is busy emptying books from the areas where they risk getting wet. I wander up to him as casually as I can, in an attempt to diffuse the awkwardness of my having returned so quickly. I have decided to keep on walking towards the city after I've gleaned the relevant information from him, so as to make it appear that I am merely passing by this time, on my way to some interesting rendezvous with friends, perhaps, when the fancy has taken me to ask him something more about the book.

"*Ciao!*" I say, and he raises his eyebrows in friendly anticipation of my query.

"I was wondering," I say, following my pre-planned script, "if you had contact details for the publishers of that novel. I have a friend in England who is a professional translator, from Italian and Spanish, and he might be able to provide an English version if they are interested. Like you say, it's a lovely story and I think it might go down well with British and American readers as well..."

"An English translation?" he says, with a strangely amused expression. "Ah no! That's not possible! This is already a translation!"

"Sorry?" I say. "You mean there's already an English translation?"

This is not good news.

"Yes. No. I mean, this book that you read, this Italian book, is already a translation. A translation from English".

I stare at him dumbly.

"The original book is written in English," he continues as I appear not to have understood. "And then it is translated to Italian. And you are reading it."

"But..." I begin slowly, piecing my thoughts together. "I have been looking on the internet and there's no evidence of any book in English of that name having been published. I can't see how..."

"No!" he interrupts. "It is written in English, but not published! Then it is translated to Italian and published. You see? The writer, he is English and he write it in English."

"He's English?" I falter. "His name... Well, I suppose it is a pseudonym, but..."

"Yes, a false name. A joke name from ancient history. There is nobody with that name today in Italy. The Englishman wants to sound like an Italian so that his book is believed to be real. It is all a part of the fiction. All a part of his imagination".

"OK, yes, well..." I say, and my deflation could hardly be more complete. "If it was written in English originally then there's hardly any point in my friend translating it all back out of Italian, is there?"

"No!" chuckles the book-seller. "I think that would be absurd! An absurd waste of your friend's time and energy that can have no benefit or interest for him or for anybody else!"

And when he laughs loudly at the very thought of this pointless endeavour, I can only laugh along with him.

I bid him goodnight, abandon the stupid ruse of pretending to walk into town and head back to the flat. I stop off at a little Indian-run grocery shop on the way in order to buy myself a comforting bottle of red wine. I come away with two, just in case...

When I get back to my room, it feels empty – until I realise that the emptiness is in fact inside me. Everything I have been doing here since I arrived is now meaningless. All those hours, all those days, weeks. Even the conversations with Sofia, her visit here. It was all built on nothing. On the desire to translate back into English something that was written in English in the first place.

I take off my plastic raincoat and hang it over the back of a chair then lie on my bed and try to imagine the strange process in which I have unwittingly been involved. How a sentence might pass out of one language, into another, and then back again. Would it remain unscathed from its journey? It seems unlikely. There are so many different ways of saying something, so many subtle nuances and hidden ambiguities that even the simplest of childlike sentences don't necessarily return from their other-tonguely experience in the same form as they left home. "The cat sat on the mat" translates literally as "*Il gatto si è seduto sul tappetino*", for example. If you feed it back into an online translator it will come back at you with the same phrase as you began with. But a human being would not necessarily do the same, if they hadn't seen the original. It could translate as "the cat sat on the rug," for instance, if you're not tuned into the English rhyme. Or "the cat was sitting on the rug".

Who knows what variations could be thrown up by the translation of a whole paragraph, a whole chapter, a whole book?

I sit up. Actually, that would interesting. To see the original English text of *Il fachiro di Firenze*. To go through it and compare it with my version. I am intrigued by the prospect. It might help me hone my translating skills as well, if I come across some mistakes. At least I would have gained some benefit from this whole ridiculous business.

I check the time. It's 4.40pm. I still have 20 minutes before the English lesson. If I run, I have time to get back to the book stall and see if he knows where I can get hold of the original English text. Putting my damp raincoat back on, I dash out of my room and nearly run right into the lady of the house. I promise her I'll be back shortly and head for the stairs outside, down which I career in a chaotic flurry, taking two at a time.

I do my best to run the whole way, but there are roads to cross, pedestrians to weave past and bicycles to avoid. And the pavements are slippery with the rain, so I cannot go too fast. When I arrive, out of breath, at the book stall I find to my dismay that it has been folded up and closed down. As I look up and down the street to see if I can spot the man himself, an elderly woman sheltering in a shop doorway notices my plight and calls out to me, gesturing past the rest of the market stalls to the street beyond. "He's just gone!" she tells me in Italian. "He lives over that way. He can't have gone far".

Thanking her, I race off again, past the rusting bikes chained to the green railings and across to the far side of the square. I look around. I can't see him in any direction. But then, just as I am about to give up, he pops out from behind a parked car at the far end of the road opposite me. I can't see his cap because he is sheltering under an umbrella, but his shorts and general body shape are distinctive enough.

He turns round as I catch him, evidently surprised to see me again. In hurried words snatched between breaths, I explain that I've been thinking some more about the book. I say that I am not sure I understood all of it in Italian and it would give me great pleasure to read the original English version. Does he know how I could lay my hands on this?

He starts to tell me that he doesn't think so, that it isn't possible, and seems in a hurry to get away from me and out of the rain. But on seeing the expression on my face, which must be a desperate sight, he relents and says he will ask someone. He pulls a phone out of a pocket and, umbrella wedged between chin and shoulder, starts to make a call. He glances up at me in a way that makes me think I should give him some privacy, so I hide from the increasingly heavy rain in the shuttered-up entrance to a small workshop while he has a conversation.

He speaks a few brief words with someone and then hangs up, keys in a new number. There then follows a longer conversation, during which he turns completely away from me so I have no clue as to what is going on. Finally, there is a fumbling in a pocket and he seems to be scribbling something down.

He crosses the road with outstretched hand. "You're in luck," he says and hands me a small slip of lined paper torn from a notebook. "This is the address of the translator, who still has the original. Maybe they will let you read it. Say that Gilberto sent you".

There is a surname – Graziani – a door number and a road name that is immediately familiar to me. *Via dell'Agnolo*. It's close to the *Murate*, the cafe where I wasted all that time on the futile fine-tuning of my pointless translation.

I thank him, tighten the hood of my plastic coat against the driving rain and head off towards the address, which thankfully isn't far from here.

When I find the right entrance, someone is just coming out of it and holds the door open for me, so I am spared the inconvenience of trying to explain the purpose of my visit through an intercom while standing in a deluge. I realise that these flats are actually part of the old convent-turned-prison itself. They must be the ones looking out over the courtyards.

Two floors up I find the appropriate door and ring. I mentally go through what I am going to say when this Signor Graziani appears.

After a few seconds there is the fumbling of a lock and the door opens up just a little to reveal a heavy purple curtain. Then the curtain is drawn back, a face appears and it belongs to Sofia.

I am so astonished that I don't know what to say. She also looks shocked.

"What are you doing here?" she demands in a fierce whisper. "It's not possible for me to talk. My brother is waiting."

My head is spinning with confusion.

"It's just..." I helplessly show her the piece of paper with her address on. "I spoke to the bookseller, Gilberto. He said there might be a translation of the *fachiro* here, I mean an original version..."

Sofia's eyes flash at me reproachfully, as if I have in some way betrayed her trust and then says: "One minute!" I am left standing on my own on the landing, dripping a small puddle on to the floor. The door is slightly ajar and through it comes the sound of a gruff male voice, followed by a few hurried words from Sofia. Through the gap between the frame and the curtain I can see a rather gloomy hallway and a door leading off it. Suddenly this is filled with the looming shape of a large bearded man with thick black body-hair, bordering on fur, spreading out from under his slightly grubby white vest up to the top of his chest, his neck, shoulders and all the way down his massive tree-trunk arms. He is glaring at me with an expression that is as far removed from friendly as is physically possible, but fortunately I am only subjected to his sulphurous scrutiny for a split-second, before he is blotted out by the return of Sofia, brandishing a sheaf of papers wrapped in a plastic carrier bag. "There!" she says. "I must go now". And with the briefest glimmer of a sad smile she pulls across the purple curtain, thuds the door shut and I hear the key turning in the lock. There is a further exchange of words inside the flat. "Orso!" I hear her call out, but beyond that I can make out nothing else.

I peel back the bag and glance at the pages, which are held together in a flimsy plastic folder. "*The Fakir of Florence*", is the heading on the front page. I got that bit right anyway, then!

Before I venture out into the road I decide it would be best to stuff the whole thing inside my coat so that there's no chance of it being spoilt by the rain. As I lope off down the road towards my lodgings, I have to keep one hand on my stomach to keep the package beneath safely in place. I must look ridiculous, but I am well beyond caring. How is it that Sofia has the original version of the book? Did she really translate it into Italian? Why, then, this pretence at helping me translate it back into English?

It's gone five o'clock when I get back. My hosts are waiting cheerfully at the dining table in the big entrance hall, notebooks and study material to hand. I have been toying with the idea of declaring myself sick so that I can get on with reading the original manuscript, but seeing them there I really can't bring myself to let them down. It can wait a couple of hours.

After the lesson and evening meal, I take a glass of water with me into my room. Then I drink it down in one gulp and refill it with some of the red wine I bought earlier. I have the feeling I am going to be needing a drink to cope with all of this.

I switch on my laptop and call up my translation then take out the sheaf of papers from Sofia. I place the book itself on the desk. My idea is to go through the two English versions, marking any significant differences on my document and referring back to the Italian text where necessary.

I start reading, my eyes flitting back and forth from paper to screen as I carefully compare the opening sentences. So far, so good! My translation has, remarkably enough, come out exactly the same as the original English!

I reach the end of the first page and this remains the case. The initial satisfaction is now rapidly being replaced by unease. This is a bit peculiar.

As I continue, my alarm grows. I start to skip sentences, paragraphs, whole pages and finally whole handfuls of pages as I desperately scan through the book in search of the smallest, slightest, most insignificant difference between my "translation" and the original *Fakir of Florence*. But my search is in vain and by the time I reach the end of the pseudo-historical account and only the final untranslated Perantulo tale remains, I have realised that the two texts are absolutely identical.

This, of course, is impossible! I pour myself another glass of corner-shop Chianti and try to imagine how this might have happened. I walk around the room and look out to the *piazza* but there is no reply in the rain. A flash of lightning over the city, somewhere near the *Duomo*, and a crack of thunder following hot on its heels.

At one point I think I have discovered the

truth of the matter. It wasn't the original version at all that Sofia gave me, but my own translation which she copied off my computer when she was here, craftily slipping in a memory stick when I was in the loo, perhaps. But I don't remember leaving the room during her brief visit. And there are more pages here than I had written at the time. She couldn't have guessed the rest of it. Unless she'd come back since, sneaked into my room in my absence... Perhaps she'd climbed onto the balcony and got in through the window!

No, this was getting more and more ridiculous. Best just drink more wine, listen to some music, try to wipe it all out of my head until the morning.

It's half past ten by the time I wake up the next day. Much later than usual. And I don't feel my usual self. I look round the bedroom and see two empty bottles of wine on the floor, surrounded by twisted remains of their wrapping and two corks, one still attached to the screw. I drank both of them! Good grief.

Then I see the pile of papers beside the computer on the desk and remember what happened. A sort of sick dread rises up inside me as I realise how far I am from the most basic understanding of what has happened here.

I flick through the papers, reading snatches of the very familiar text which I thought was the result of my painstaking translation work but which turns out to be – what exactly?

Then I pick up the book itself, *Il fachiro di Firenze*, and gaze at the cover portrait of the man with the dagger sticking out of his chest, which I assumed was a much later depiction of the central figure himself. Since he never existed, it can't be though. So who is he? Where does this piece of art come from?

All of a sudden, despite or perhaps because of the effect on my brain of last night's alcohol, I make a connection that I haven't made before. I lurch towards the wardrobe in search of my phone, which I have barely used since I arrived here.

I only have a few images saved on there and I quickly scroll through to find the one I have in mind. Just after a gruesome skeleton heaving himself out of his tomb, I find him – the figure on the front of the book. The portrait is one of the few cultural sights of Florence that I snapped, within half an hour of arriving in the city, in the little church near the station, before I abandoned the folly of photography.

There he is now, familiar to me now from four weeks of working on the book. Those fine, intelligent features, light beard and a rather stoical, knowing expression. When I took the photo I didn't even notice the dagger and the bloodstain on his monk-like cowl – like all the other stupid tourists, I was so busy lining up my shot that I saw nothing with my own eyes. That must have been why I was immediately attracted to the book on the stall, I conclude. I had seen the face before and it had sunk down into my unconscious mind, from where it called out to me in self-recognition when I caught a glimpse of the cover.

Comparing the two images, I notice something else a bit odd. The bottom of my photo is slightly spoiled by the reflection of the flash on the oil of the painting. The version on the cover of the book, although it is cropped a little tighter, shows the beginning of the same blemish. Were both images taken from exactly the same angle?

And who was he, this man? Was he a real murder victim or an artist's model, representing somebody else, some historical figure or saint? Maybe I should go back to the *Chiesa di San Paolini* and try to find out some more about him?

I idly flick through to the next image and nearly drop the phone in shock. It is Sofia. No, it is the other portrait from the church, the last thing I took before I put my phone-camera away. But it is, nevertheless, Sofia. She may be disguised here as a long-passed saint or Madonna, but there is absolutely no mistaking her slender and delicate face, lit up with the faintest of half-sad half-smiles.

I am breaking into a cold sweat. My legs feel so weak that I am not sure that I will be able to stand up.

Looking down again at the picture I am overwhelmed by the quiet power of this unassuming holy woman, gazing towards a dream of the eternal infinite. I have to see her. I have to talk to her. I have to know what all this means.

I get ready and leave the flat without even bothering to make myself a coffee. Helped by the fug of a hangover, I have completely abandoned any attempt at a rational resolution of this puzzle. I just have the physical need to get into the open air, to move through the streets, to run and to run and to find my way to Sofia.

Yesterday's rain has passed and bright early autumn sunlight is swept into my face by a fresh breeze.

I am feeling uplifted by the new single-mindedness that is propelling me towards the *Murate*, blindly joyful that some kind of resolution lies ahead of me, even though I cannot imagine the form that it might take and my enthusiasm whisks me swiftly to Sofia's street, past the cleaner who has the street entrance propped open, and back up to the door at which I rung last night.

The lock turns, the curtain is drawn back but this time it is the brother who is standing there. He doesn't look particularly pleased to see me.

"*Buongiorno!*" I say. "Could I speak to Sofia, please?"

He recoils slightly, eyebrows raised in a sardonic expression.

"Sofia?" he repeats. "So you want to see Sofia?"

"Yes," I reply simply. Knowing that this is Sofia's flat and he's only living here because of her automatic kindness to a sibling, I don't feel the need to explain myself any further.

He turns away from the door, while still holding it firmly with one massive arm, as if making it entirely clear that I am not invited to come in.

"Sofia!" he calls.

"*Si*, Orso?" comes a strangely subdued female voice from within.

"There is someone here to see you!" he replies.

There is the sound of muttering and movement inside and then a woman appears behind him in the hallway. Only it is not Sofia. It is the other woman who sometimes works with her at the cafe below, the nervous and unsmiling one. She looks completely confused to see me. Frightened, even.

"Oh, I'm sorry," I say. "I didn't mean you... I meant the other Sofia who lives here".

She makes a strange whimpering noise under her breath and the man breathes in and puffs himself up to his full gigantic size.

"There is only one Sofia here, *Signor*", he announces. "And that is my wife".

And, with that, he slams the door shut in my face.

Immediately from within I hear the woman's voice, protesting and wailing, and angry rebukes in response.

I don't want to hang around. I don't like this at all. I'm getting out of here.

I run back to the flat. I don't jog, or make haste with intermittent sprints. I run flat out all the way.

And when I get back to the room, I immediately grab the English text of *Il fachiro*. Not my translation because it's on the computer, but the one that Sofia gave me. The one that I thought Sofia gave me. And it doesn't even matter which text it is because they are both exactly the same.

I quickly find the section I am looking for: "The preacher had been stabbed... ambushed by a man known locally as Orso, rumoured to be the long-lost husband of Sister Sophia of *Le Murate*".

Orso – the man known by the Italian word for "bear". The man who just opened the door to me. I immediately start packing my bag. I begin with my laptop and my books and then stuff everything in after it, as quickly as I possibly can. I dash over to the bathroom and grab my belongings from there.

I still have two days left of my stay in Florence, in theory, but I am not going to be seeing them through. I will have to give some explanation to my hosts as I leave, but frankly I don't care what they think about it. I don't have a ticket to go home today, but that doesn't matter. I am going to go to the station and get a train out of Florence. Any train. Without waiting to buy a ticket. I'll pay a fine if necessary. It doesn't matter. All that I care about is not being here anymore.

I am having trouble doing up my bag. I haven't packed it carefully enough and it doesn't all fit. I push it closed, pull harder at the fastener and the whole zip breaks. Telling myself to calm down, to keep in control, I go to the window for a brief gulp of air. And there below, climbing out of a small bright blue car, I see an enormously bulky figure in a white-grey vest, clutching a small pink scrap of paper. It is Orso. Now he is studying the writing on the paper. There is something long and bulky showing on the outside of his right leg, concealed beneath his combat trousers. Some sort of knife, perhaps. A dagger. At that moment he looks up and sees me, his dark and angry eyes boring into me like lethal lasers. He stuffs the pink paper into his pocket and heads directly for the front door to the flats.

I panic. I grab my bag, gaping open as it is,

and start to leave my room, before I realise that my passport is still on the bedside table and I have to go back and get it.

As I do so, I hear the buzz of the intercom from below and, as I skid out into the dining room hallway, I see that the lady of the house is answering it. She looks round at me, smiling, and says "*si*" to the caller in the street below.

I have no time. I have no time to explain all this to her, to tell her not to let him in, to tell her that he wants to kill me.

I have to get out of here, I have to get away, and now my exit has been blocked by Orso's arrival. It might just be possible to get down the stairs while he's coming up in the lift, or vice versa, but that's far too risky. My life is at stake.

The only answer is the emergency exit, the escape out through the kitchen balcony and down into the "canyon" of the higgledy-piggledy space between the back of the buildings.

Despite the urgency of the situation, I'd like to say goodbye to my hosts, to thank them for their many kindnesses, wish them well for the future. But I can't. I don't want to alert anyone to what I am about to do. They'd only try to stop me. Or inadvertently let Orso know where I was. I just have to get on with it.

I rush out on to the balcony and look down. This escape route doesn't look so easy now that I actually have to try it! I decide that my best bet is to drop down on to some veranda roofing, then use a ventilation shaft to climb down the next storey and into the passageway at the bottom. From there, I should be able to get into the back of the shops and out into the street.

I drop my bag down ahead of me and already there is an ominous sign – the roofing cracks slightly under its weight. Under the weight of my bag, not of my body! But this is no time for hesitation, so I lower myself down off the balcony until I am dangling as close as I can to the fragile material below and then let go. There is an almighty crash, which must be alerting the whole of the block to what I am doing, but the roof holds firm. I crawl across to the edge and sling my bag down the next stage before wrapping my arms around the thick ventilation shaft and trying to glide down to the ground. No sooner have I started, though, than it pulls away from the wall in a great puff of brick dust and plaster and I plummet backwards with it. Afraid of being crushed, I leap free and there is thudding moment of darkness during which I think I lose consciousness. As I try to get to my feet, I realise there is a hideous searing pain in my right ankle, which seems incapable of taking any weight. I must have broken it. Shit.

As I hobble around in the duct-debris for my bag, I am aware of voices all around and above me. I glance up and there are boggle-eyed faces filling what seems to be every single window and balcony overlooking the yard. Two floors above I see my host and Orso looking down at me and gesticulating.

There is no time to lose! I negotiate the one remaining level, helped by the presence of a grimy but reasonably solid plastic table on to which I gingerly lower myself. Then I limp off, as fast as I can despite the agony, past bin bags and abandoned pushchairs, until I reach a door into a kitchen area. I fling myself through it and out the other side, where I immediately collide with a man carrying a huge tray of fancy pastries. He shouts out in outraged fury, as half a dozen of them fall on to me, smearing my hair and shoulders with cream. I push on and emerge into the polished perfection of what I immediately recognise as the *pasticceria* round the corner from the flat. The man with the cakes has come after me and is grabbing my arm, but I swing my bag in his face, causing him to career backwards and fall on to the nearest table, sending drinks flying into the air and sprinkling a pair of well-dressed middle-aged Florentine ladies with cappuccino froth. Amidst the shrieking, shattering chaos, I break through the queue of bewildered customers into the street where, as luck would have it, a taxi has just dropped off a fare. I climb in, ask for the railway station and, despite a severe glance in the direction of my cream-splattered upper body, the driver heads off with me on board. He may catch a glimpse in his wing mirror of the fist-waving cake-shop man coming after me, but he chooses to pretend he has seen nothing.

As we make our way through the city traffic, I dab at myself with some tissue, trying to get rid of the cream, but end up making it worse and smearing it more deeply into my clothing. During the *pasticceria* incident I forgot how much my ankle hurts, but now it is reminding me with a vengeance. The same leg has also been cut further up. There is a rip in my trousers and a deep red stain spreading down from the knee.

During the short ride across the city, I catch sight of many familiar landmarks that I've walked past or visited during my stay, but none of them seem real any more. They are like images on a rapidly-turning merry-go-round, disappearing almost before they have arrived, spiralling down a plughole and dragging with them all the experiences, all the insights, all the energies that have touched me here.

Amidst all this, two emotions keep forcing themselves into my mind. One is a sense of endless loss for Sofia, whose very existence seems to have been swept out of my hands just as I was reaching out to touch her. The other is a deep and gnawing fear that Orso will catch up with me before I can leave the city.

From time to time, I look out of the back window of the taxi and, on one chilling occasion, I am sure I see his bulky figure in his tiny blue car only five or six places behind me in the queue of traffic. Fortunately, he is stopped by some lights and I don't see him again, but when we reach the station I am still horribly aware of his possible proximity. I thrust a banknote at the driver, call out my thanks and throw myself towards the platforms. Once I reach the concourse I don't even want to stop to check the departures board for the first train out of town and, as I run and read at the same time, I knock into a man cutting across in front of me from a platform.

I carry on regardless, as there is a train leaving for Torino in a couple of minutes, but something makes me glance back at him for a moment. He looks angry with me, as if I was to blame for the collision, but there's something else there as well that frightens me. I don't know what. A shadow passes between us and then his face is quickly forgotten as it merges into the kaleidoscopic chaos of my pain-fevered imagination and I leave Florence for ever.

THE WHIRLING DANCE

Once during Perantulo's wanderings, after he had fled the final collapse of the great Thopic Empire in the east, he came to the land of Lytia and entered a city of increasing renown by the name of Arnovi.

Built in a fertile river valley and site on a main road to the Lytian capital, Viticani, Arnovi had built its wealth on trade and on the exchange of money, with branches of its famous banks spread across the known world. Furthermore, the wealthy rulers of the city prided themselves on their artistic sensibilities and on an elevated spirituality. They took great delight in commissioning translations of the great metaphysical works from Thopia, Beziz, Khaluvia, Mesqa-Murro and beyond, which they combined with the religious beliefs of Lytia itself to produce a system of thought that appeared both broader and deeper than that of their ancestors.

It was thus with great interest that the merchant-princes of Arnovi learnt of the presence within their walls of the famed sage, Perantulo, and before he had been in town more than seven hours he found himself invited to a banquet at which were gathered the leading members of all the most important families of that community.

Perantulo politely refused the large part of the opulent spread placed before him, though he did permit himself to eat goat's cheese, bread and figs and to drink plenty of his hosts' red wine, which was, of course, of a very high quality. Throughout the meal, he kept the Arnovian arriviste-aristocrats entertained with accounts of his travels in far-off lands and of his encounters with fishermen, sultans, magicians, warriors, hermits, princesses and child prodigies.

After the assembled dignitaries and their wives and lovers had laughed with particular heartiness at his tale of the fearful spider who tried to spin a web to save the moon from sinking into the sea, there fell a sudden contented silence. Perantulo thought to himself that this was maybe the moment to thanks his hosts and depart, for in truth he never felt fully at ease in the company of those who stack their self-esteem to the same toppling heights as their hoarded coins.

But just as he drew a breath to speak, another voice struck up from the other side of the room, at the head of the principal table. It was Misoco De Mici, the money-exchanger who was the *de facto* ruler of Arnovi.

"I wonder, O Wise Man, if I might ask you for some advice of a personal nature?" he said, lounging back in his ornate padded chair. "Although not of such a personal nature that I cannot speak of it in front of three score guests!" he added, to a ripple of amusement.

Misoco took out from his money belt a golden coin of that city, known as an arnile. "This arnile," he said, "has two sides, as you may know. On one side here, we have the Rose of Arnovi, the symbol of all the prestige, achievement and physical greatness for which our city has become known. On the other side is a wandering holy man who is usually named as Oravius but could very easily, my friend, be you!"

There was another murmur of delight from the other diners.

"Now these two sides of the coin are each as much a part of the coin as the other. And yet when one beholds one side one cannot behold, at the same time, the other. Even when I hold the coin thus, with its outer rim facing me, I cannot see both sides simultaneously. And so it is that he who sees the holiness of one side of the coin cannot see the glory of the other. Likewise – and this, O Perantulo, is what concerns me in particular – when someone sees the pomp and richness of the Rose of Arnovi they cannot see that behind this lies the holiness of the man of spirit. How can this be resolved, do you think?"

Perantulo smiled. "The question has a deeper significance than my host perhaps realises," he said. "For it touches upon the essentially dual aspect of human existence itself – at one and the same time we are both mere flesh aspiring upwards to divine purity and yet also divine purity yearning downwards for the incarnation-in-flesh that enables it to act out its will on earth".

Misoco smiled. He was happy with this metaphysical extension of his dilemma.

Perantulo took a swig of red wine and looked up for a moment at the sumptuous fresco depicting a winged cherub on the ceiling of the dining hall.

And then he said: "The problem, O Patron of the Arts, is one of essence. The essence of the coin, that which gives it its value, is gold. But this essence is corrupted by the form which it takes".

"Corrupted?" asked Misoco, with a slight frown. "How so?"

"Inherent in the existence of the coin is pride. Pride in Arnovi, pride in the wealth associated with possession of the coin. This pride is most obviously reflected in the side of the coin showing the Rose of Arnovi. This represents, as you said, all the pomp of the city and its culture. But it is also there in the other side, depicting the holy man. Here is the pride of somehow rising above the material level of merchant life. But it is an ostentatious pride, that has to have itself imprinted on every arnile coming out of the mint. It is a worse kind of pride, because it is pride that is pretending that it is not pride at all, but holiness. It is a dangerous kind of pride, because it is a pride that would reduce the spirit to nothing but a fig leaf for the base lust for wealth. There is no upwards aspiration at all on this side of the coin, only another form of downwards movement, from the pursuit of material power to the pursuit of power by the hypocritical means of an insincere interest in divine purity. The true holy man would no more adorn the face of a usurer's coin than speak apologies for his greed!"

Perantulo pushed back his chair and stood up, to gasps of astonishment from the guests.

"There is only one way to see the essence of the coin beyond this corruption and to achieve the reconciliation of the two contrasting sides which are inherent to its form," he added, fixing the open-mouthed Misoco with a fierce gaze. "But I suspect it would be far too dangerous for someone like you".

The merchant-prince was caught in two minds. On the one hand, this ragged old man had more or less accused him to his face of the sin of usury and he should have him thrown out of the city. On the other hand he knew, deep down, that there was a contradiction between his own wealth and spiritual aspiration. That was why he had asked the question and that was why he would still very much like to hear the response.

"Very well, O Strange Savant," he said at length. "Show us what you have in mind. None of us have anything to fear from a brittle-boned old guru such as you!"

There were guffaws of mirth from the

other guests – as much out of relief as anything, for they had been alarmed by the tone of Perantulo's reply and by his warning of danger. Misoco's dismissive quip had, as he had intended, succeeded in dispelling some of the power that the sage was increasingly exerting over the room.

Perantulo walked over to Misoco's table with outstretched hand. "The coin, please," he said.

When he had taken it, he told Misoco: "This works better if you go on your knees, so that your face is level with the tabletop".

The merchant was not as young and supple as he had once been, but he managed to sink down to his knees and those gathered did likewise, or stood crouching to see over the heads of those in front of them.

Then Perantulo took the gold arnile, placed it on its edge on the wooden surface and, with a nimble flick of finger and thumb, set it spinning.

"There," he said. "Both sides are visible at once, and yet also invisible. It is the essence of the gold that shines through the doubled artifice of the coin".

People began to stand up again, a little disappointed in the demonstration.

One fellow, a wool merchant who hoped

to impress Misoco by taking up the dismissive tone of his earlier comment, burst out: "That's all very clever. A nice little party trick from a wily old conjuror, but you were showing signs of senile confusion with that warning you gave us! A coin spinning on a table is hardly a danger to anyone, you fear-mongering falsifier!"

There was a great uproar of amused approval from most of the well-fed bourgeoisie. Only Misoco himself remained silent and straight-faced.

Perantulo drew himself indignantly to his full height and faced the wool-trader.

"You," he declared, "are confusing representation with reality! Unless I am very much mistaken, this coin has never been the real subject of our discussion. Is this not the case, Misoco?"

Misoco nodded thoughtfully. "Yes, that is so," he said. "I suppose that there is another level at which I might now participate, if I dare?"

"Indeed," said Perantulo, smiling at the rich man's understanding. "But first!" he announced with a wave of his hand, "we must clear a space!"

When the tables had all been moved to the edges of the room, and the guests had lined up in front of them in a circle, only

Perantulo and Misoco remained at the centre.

"Now I will show you how to spin like the coin!" the sage shouted gleefully to the merchant and slowly he began to turn on the spot. Step by step he picked up the pace. His eyes were shut, both his arms were raised in the air and the bottom of his woollen robe started to lift as he span.

Perantulo whirled. His whirling was so powerful that it made the air spin round in the room. Some guests had their hats blown off and the women's hair was swept into disarray. Dishes and glasses trembled and knocked against each other. One stack of fruit bowls, piled up a little hastily as the room was being cleared, toppled to the ground with a great shattering. Merchants' papers – for banquets such as this were a useful occasion for doing business – were whisked up into the air and twirled round and round in the great current of circulation caused by the gyrating guru. The guests started grasping hold of table legs and pillars for fear of being unbalanced by the wind and they exchanged anxious glances with each other. They hoped Perantulo would stop, but he didn't. Now a real whirlwind was blowing up. The doors to the room flew off their hinges and the glass shattered in the fancy windows high up near the ceiling. There was a crashing and a splintering from beyond the room as the ornate furniture, vases, sculptures and paintings in the merchant's palace were hurled into the air, against walls and on to the floor. The roof lifted off, splintered into pieces and crashed into the surrounding streets. The fabric of the building started to give way, but still Perantulo whirled, now under a moonless star-specked night sky. The hurricane gathered more speed, more force and now it was attacking the other homes in the wealthy part of Arnovi. It spread to the shopping streets around Rose Square, crashed through the windows and pulled all the fine silks, spices, perfumes and sugared delicacies out into the night. It rushed down chimneys and stole the flames, spreading them across the city as it went. The Tower of Magnificence was tilted over by the force of the wind, hanging there in improbable leaning suspension for several minutes before smashing down into smithereens in the park below. People ran everywhere to escape the devastation and somehow they all avoided harm. The great whirling only seemed to want to destroy the bricks and mortar of Arnovi, the structures of its vanity, and not the humanity who lived there. Now the wind was howling like a banshee and flames were rushing to fill the spaces that it left. The townsfolk looked up to see that even the Great Dome itself, decorated with enormous rose-patterns in green, pink and white marble, had been caught up in the madness. Flames were licking up its sides and, all of a sudden, it completely collapsed in on itself in a great implosion of dust and glowing ashes.

Suddenly, it all stopped. There was no wind. All was silent apart from the crackling of the fires that were finishing off the ruins of the city. Perantulo was standing still amidst the rubble of the merchant's palace, still surrounded by the same audience. He opened his eyes.

"We are beginning to strip away that which separates you from your self" he said to Misoco, who had remained completely still throughout the chaos. "Will you join me now or are you too afraid of what you might find?"

"I have nothing to be afraid of," said the merchant calmly. "Begin your spinning again and this time take me with you".

So Perantulo whirled again. And his whirling was so forceful that Misoco could not have stopped himself from joining in, even if he had wanted to. Perantulo's whirling was like a magnetic centrifuge from which nobody could escape. The other guests found themselves spinning, too, their arms lifting and their clothing billowing. Even the wretched wool merchant, who was now bitterly regretting the derision he had directed at the mage, was caught up in the great gyration. Outside in the streets the people forgot their bewilderment at all that had happened and became hypnotised by the turning that was induced in them by Perantulo. As they turned, they blurred. The ruined city blurred. Cats, dogs, pigeons, sparrows, rats and wall-lizards also started turning and blurring. None of them knew where they were any more, none of them knew who they were any more. There were no borders to universal being. All was one enormous rotation.

"It's working!" shouted Misoco. "The sides have gone, the coin has gone! There is only the golden blur, the churning of the Oneness!"

"We are not there yet!" cried Perantulo. "We must go faster, faster, faster!"

And with that he doubled the speed of his whirling, tripled it, then multiplied it beyond the imagination of the sharpest mathematician. Perantulo whirled at such a speed that he caught up the passing of time itself, overtook it and then looped right round to approach it from behind, like the snake that devours its own tail. And then this hoop of time likewise began to spin, faster and ever faster, until it too had become a blur like the golden coin on the tabletop and until the vanity of its fake structure could no longer hide the all-embracing glory of its infinite and eternal fire.

Non-fiction from Winter Oak

FORMS OF FREEDOM

PAUL CUDENEC

In this philosophical work, the author of *The Anarchist Revelation* and *The Stifled Soul of Humankind* challenges layer upon layer of the assumptions that lie largely unchallenged beneath contemporary industrial capitalist society. He rejects limited definitions of freedom as an absence of specific restraints in favour of a far deeper and more radical analysis which describes individual, collective, planetary and metaphysical levels of freedom.

"How can the human race embrace freedom if it does not have a clear idea of what freedom *is*? How can we ever gain a clear idea of freedom if we do not even start *looking* for it in the right places?"

Non-fiction from Winter Oak

THE STIFLED SOUL OF HUMANKIND

PAUL CUDENEC

Paul Cudenec depicts a humanity dispossessed, a society in which freedom, autonomy, creativity, culture, and the spirit of collective solidarity have been deliberately suffocated by a ruthlessly violent and exploitative elite. But he also identifies an underground current of heresy and resistance which resurfaces at key moments in history and which, he argues, has the primal strength to carry us forward to a future of vitality and renewal.

"We have to reintroduce ourselves to history, not as observers but as participants. The power that we can rediscover in ourselves is, among other things, the power to create the future. Prophecy brings hope, hope brings courage, courage brings action, action brings inspiration, inspiration brings more determination, renewed hope, deepened courage. Once this magical spiral of revolt has started spinning, it takes on a life of its own".

Non-fiction from Winter Oak

THE ANARCHIST REVELATION

PAUL CUDENEC

Paul Cudenec draws on an impressively wide range of authors to depict a corrupted civilization on the brink of self-destruction and to call for a powerful new philosophy of resistance and renewal. He combines the anarchism of the likes of Gustav Landauer, Michael Bakunin and Herbert Read with the philosophy of René Guénon, Herbert Marcuse and Jean Baudrillard; the existentialism of Karl Jaspers and Colin Wilson; the vision of Carl Jung, Oswald Spengler and Idries Shah, and the environmental insight of Derrick Jensen and Paul Shepard in a work of ideological alchemy fuelled by the ancient universal esoteric beliefs found in Sufism, Taoism and hermeticism.

"The least pessimistic book I can recall reading. It brings anarchist resistance and the spirit together in a very wide-ranging and powerful contribution". John Zerzan, author of *Future Primitive* and *Running on Emptiness*.

Non-fiction from Winter Oak

ANTIBODIES, ANARCHANGELS & OTHER ESSAYS

PAUL CUDENEC

Antibodies, Anarchangels and Other Essays brings together a selection of work by Paul Cudenec in which he calls for a new deeper level of resistance to global capitalism – one which is rooted in the collective soul. He leads us along the intertwining environmental and philosophical strands of *Antibodies*, through the passion of *Anarchangels* and *The Task* and on to an informative analysis of Gladio, a state-terrorist branch of what he terms the "plutofascist" system. Also included, alongside short pieces on Taoism and Jungian psychology, is an interview with the author, in which he explains key aspects of his approach.

"Very readable and profoundly thoughtful... Many new insights on the destructive relationship between the greater part of humanity and the planet which tries to sustain them". Peter Marshall, author of *Demanding the Impossible: A History of Anarchism*.

RICHARD JEFFERIES: HIS LIFE AND HIS IDEALS

HENRY S. SALT

"He was a pagan, a pantheist, a worshipper of earth and sea, and of the great sun 'burning in the heaven'; he yearned for a free, natural, fearless life of physical health and spiritual exaltation, and for a death in harmony with the life that preceded it."

So is the writer Richard Jefferies (1848-1887) described by Henry S. Salt in this study first published in 1894. The book sparked controversy at the time, as Salt – a campaigner for animal rights, vegetarianism and socialism – used it to claim Jefferies for one of his own, highlighting the social radicalism and nature-based spirituality in his subject's later writing. He demolishes the conservative presentation of Jefferies as a mere chronicler of country life and reveals him as a flawed yet inspirational figure whose best works were "unsurpassed as prose poems by anything which the English language contains".

Non-fiction from Winter Oak

THE STORY OF MY HEART

RICHARD JEFFERIES

"Having drunk deeply of the heaven above and felt the most glorious beauty of the day, and remembering the old, old, sea, which (as it seemed to me) was but just yonder at the edge, I now became lost, and absorbed into the being or existence of the universe. I felt down deep into the earth under, and high above into the sky, and farther still to the sun and stars. Still farther beyond the stars into the hollow of space, and losing thus my separateness of being came to seem like a part of the whole".

Richard Jefferies' masterpiece of prose-poetry expresses his sublime yearning not just for connection with nature but for spiritual transcendence. This new Winter Oak edition includes a preface by writer Paul Cudenec exploring the significance of Jefferies' work against a backdrop of disillusionment with industrial civilization and a cultural urge for the regeneration of human society.

MORE INFORMATION

To get in touch with Winter Oak please email
winteroak@greenmail.net or go to our website at
www.winteroak.org.uk.